The Perfect Loophole

A. K. Gentry

Brushy Mountain Publications

ISBN Paperback: 979-8-9888618-2-9

ISBN Digital: 979-8-9888618-3-6

Library of Congress Number: 2023923174

Printed in the United States of America

Brushy Mountain Publications, Statesville, North Carolina

CONTENTS

Chapter 1

Angela Sutton zipped her carry-on bag. Having already checked in online for her flight, she took the hotel's courtesy van to the airport. Angela had come to Long Beach, California, for a job interview. According to the news, the huge toy company, M & L Toys, was moving their headquarters to Charlotte, North Carolina, and they were advertising jobs in all the departments of the business. Angela was interested in marketing.

Currently employed by a small snack food company based in Durham, Angela was hoping to get the job and move back home. Her parents were still on the family farm northeast of Charlotte, which was about 100 miles from Durham. Angela was an only child and missed her parents. Plus, the lifestyle of living in the country was more appealing to her than life in a city, and she could easily commute to Charlotte from the farm.

On her way to the airport, Angela realized that she was glad to be leaving the stress of crowds, traffic and dealing with an unknown area. She couldn't wait to get back to what was familiar and the peace of being on the farm. The van dropped her off at the departures area, and Angela went straight to security. The line was not extremely long, and fifteen minutes later, she was sitting at her gate.

*****

Michael Jamison looked around his condominium in Long Beach. He had been comfortable here, but he knew it was now time to leave. Michael had moved to Long Beach from Los Angeles with his family when he was a child. His uncles, Max and Louis Niche, had moved their company, M & L Toys, to Long Beach hoping there would be less congestion. That is how it was in the very beginning, but now, even Long Beach felt as crowded and developed as Los Angeles did. Recently, though, Max and Louis had retired and given the company to Michael. It was his responsibility to keep the company operating smoothly and earning a profit.

Michael's family had lived in California for five generations. He liked California and hated to leave, but he finally reached the limit of his willingness to endure the constantly increasing cost of doing business and began to scour the country for a place to relocate.

Michael's administrative assistant would meet the movers on Monday to make sure everything was packed and loaded onto the moving company's truck. He had already driven some of his belongings to Charlotte where he had bought a house on Lake Norman. Leaving his car there, Michael had flown back to Long Beach to finish the process of moving his company out of the state.

A taxi dropped Michael off at the departures entrance of the airport. He went through the line to check a bag then made it easily through security. Michael found a seat at his gate, took out his phone and began to check his emails. He had only replied to two when the boarding process started.

The toy company was successful, and Michael could afford a first-class seat. However, he chose to upgrade to business class because frugality was a habit he learned from his mother and her brothers when the company was small and just getting started.

*****

Angela heard her zone call to board. She picked up her carry-on bag and got in line. This jet had rows of three seats on one side and two seats on the other. She was glad she could get a seat on the side with smaller rows, but she had to upgrade to business class to get it. Looking at her ticket, Angela found her seat and opened the compartment above it to store her bag.

Struggling with the bag, Angela heard a male voice saying, "Here, let me help you."

Angela looked to her right and saw a tall, lean man with dark hair, dark eyes, and a wide, captivating smile. He was possibly the most handsome man she had ever seen.

"Thank you," she said as she smiled and tried to hide her blushing attraction to the man.

When Michael heard the woman thank him, he looked at her and blinked. There was something about her. She looked naturally attractive without a lot of makeup, which was different from the women he usually associated with. She had long, nondescript dark blond hair, gray eyes, and a dabbling of freckles across her nose. But her smile. That smile grabbed his attention. Her whole face smiled, and her eyes sparkled.

Michael felt drawn to her in a way he could not describe.

"You're welcome," he said.

Michael watched the woman sit in the window seat of the row below where he was standing. His seat was the one beside her. He wasn't sure if this was luck or fate. All he knew was that this woman had instantly captured his attention, and he was excited to get to know her. Noticing the line of passengers behind him, Michael took his seat.

CHAPTER 2

Michael sat in his assigned seat and fastened his seatbelt. Once he was comfortably settled, he turned to Angela.

"Where are you headed?" he asked her.

"Charlotte. And you?" she asked politely.

"I'm going to Charlotte, too," he said, smiling. "Do you live there?" He was hoping she would say yes.

"No. I currently live in Durham," Angela answered. "My family lives not too far north of Charlotte, so I left my car at their house. They'll pick me up, and I will drive back to Durham tomorrow. Do you live in Charlotte?"

"I do now," he said. "I'm moving there. It's time to get out of California."

"I've heard that from a lot of people lately," Angela replied with a nod. "I think you'll like the

Charlotte area."

"Why were you in Long Beach?" he asked.

"I had a job interview," she replied.

"Are you trying to move to California?" he asked, creasing his brow in slight confusion.

Angela rolled her eyes and shook her head, "No! If that were the case, I would not have applied. The company I hope to get a job with is moving to Charlotte. If I get the job, I can move back home, plus it will be more of a challenge than what I do now."

"Where do you work now?" Michael asked.

"I'm the sole marketing, public relations, and sales staff for a snack food company in Durham," she replied. "It's a good job, don't get me wrong, but it's local. M & L Toys, which is where I applied, is global. I find that appealing."

Michael blinked, stunned. She had interviewed for a job in his company.

"Well," he said, "I hope you get the job."

"Thank you. What do you do for a living?" Angela asked.

In a split second, Michael decided not to divulge that he owned M & L Toys.

"I'm in sales, so I travel a lot," he answered. "I'm moving to Charlotte because the cost of living is slightly lower, and the taxes are a lot lower."

Angela laughed. He loved the sound of her laugh. It was spontaneous, joyful, and infectious.

"That's another thing I hear from everyone who moves to my state," she replied.

Michael grinned. "When do you expect to hear from your interview?"

"I'm not sure of the timing, but if I get a letter, I didn't get the job. If I get a call, I'll be given a start date." She paused then said, "Honestly, I would love to work there. I liked what I saw in the short time I was at their office. Everyone smiled and looked satisfied with their jobs, but I can't imagine they would all move to Charlotte."

Angela paused briefly and gave Michael a squinty look.

He was amused and asked, "What?"

"Tell me what you like to do," she said. "I'll tell you the best places in the Charlotte area to do them."

"OK," Michael said. "I like to go boating and fishing."

"You're in luck. Lake Norman and Lake Wiley are both close to Charlotte. What else?"

"How about snow skiing?" he asked.

"There are several ski slopes in the Boone

area," Angela answered. "They're tame compared to what's out west, but they're nice. West Virginia has some great resorts if you don't mind the drive to get there."

Michael smiled. He already knew the answers to his questions, but he wanted to hear what she had to say. Her eyes lit up and sparkled while she talked. He wondered what they looked like when she was sad then quickly decided he didn't want to find out.

A few hours later, both Michael and Angela looked up in surprise when they realized they were on the final approach to St Louis.

Michael smiled, "I do believe this is the first time that I haven't been bored on a flight. Thank you. I'm Michael Jamison."

"I don't fly often, but I truly enjoyed talking with you, Michael. My name is Angela Sutton. I'm sure it would be too big of a coincidence if we were on the same flight to Charlotte and have seats together. I'm quite spoiled," she said grinning.

"Me, too," Michael replied, smiling.

When the plane landed and stopped at the gate, the door opened, and people gathered in the aisle to disembark. Michael stood slightly behind their seats and retrieved Angela's bag.

He allowed her to get out of the seat, stand in front of him and receive her bag.

"Thank you," she said, smiling.

"You're welcome," he replied smiling back at her.

The line in front of them started moving. They walked through the door of the plane, onto the jet bridge, then to the monitors inside.

"I'm at gate B12," Michael said.

Angela laughed, "Me, too! I guess we're on the same flight after all."

Michael and Angela moved along the maze of people as they walked through the airport and found their gate. Boarding would start in fifteen minutes.

"Oh!" Angela said, "I'm glad our flight wasn't late. This is a short layover."

Michael was beginning to wish they had missed this flight. He would like to spend more time with Angela. He found her fascinating. He knew they wouldn't be sitting together on the next flight. It was a small commuter jet with two seats on one side and one seat on the other. He had a seat in the row of single seats.

When everyone had boarded, Michael looked back two rows to see Angela settling into the window seat. He saw the seat beside her was empty. Michael admitted to himself that he liked Angela and wanted to continue traveling with her. He stood then approached the flight attendant.

Pointing to Angela's seat, he said, "I'm traveling with the woman in that row. I would like to sit with her. If someone comes and tries to claim the seat, I'm more than happy to let that person have my seat."

The attendant smiled and told him to go ahead and change seats because the plane was not completely full.

Michael walked back and sat down beside Angela.

"Surprise!" he said.

Angela smiled then laughed.

"You're crazy!" she exclaimed softly. "You gave up your single seat with all that leg room to come back here?"

"Yeah," Michael said, "but you're back here. It would've been boring up there."

"I'm glad you moved," Angela said, grinning. "It would've been boring back here, too."

Michael laughed. They continued to talk through the flight to Charlotte. They discussed everything from hobbies to food to music. Both felt a need to get to know the other before the flight ended.

Michael usually carried two types of business cards. One had the company name and logo. The other had only his name and phone number. When the final approach to the Charlotte airport was announced, Michael took two business cards from his pocket. They did not have the company logo.

"You're my only friend in North Carolina," he said as he handed her both cards. "This is my phone number. Would you mind putting your number on the back of the other card? If it's OK with you, I would love to call just to talk."

Angela smiled, and without hesitation, she took the card and wrote her phone number on the back.

"You may call anytime," she assured him.

After the plane landed, the two walked along the jet bridge and into the terminal. Then they walked together to the baggage claim area.

"It was very nice meeting you, Michael. I hope you'll be glad you moved here," she said and held up her phone. "The parents are outside the door, so I need to go."

"I enjoyed meeting you, too," Michael said. "Let me know when you come back to visit your parents. Maybe we can meet for dinner."

Angela smiled, "I would like that." She paused then added, "Very much." Angela turned and walked to the door, turned back and waved, then left.

Michael felt a slight sense of sadness when Angela left the building. Never in his life had he been so instantly taken with a woman. It didn't matter if she was employed by M & L Toys or not; he was determined to get to know her. He would call human resources first thing Monday and find out the status of her application.

*****

Angela was content to spend the rest of the June weekend on the farm with her parents. They had a close relationship and enjoyed each others' company. Plus, riding around the farm on an ATV or her horse was an automatic stress reliever.

Sunday, the family had returned from church and was eating lunch. Angela felt relaxed and at peace.

Ray, her father, said, "Angela, if the weather's good, do you think you could come home next weekend? The wheat is ready, and the harvest will go faster if there are three of us working."

"Sure, Dad," Angela replied. "I can do that. I'll come home Thursday regardless of the weather."

The one thing Angela really liked about her current job was that she could work longer hours four days a week and take Fridays off, which made it easy to return to the farm to help her parents on the weekends.

Later that afternoon, Angela's SUV was packed and ready to go. She hugged her parents goodbye and told them that she would see them Thursday evening. By the time Angela got to the interstate, the Sunday evening traffic was heavy and sometimes slow. Angela used the time to reflect on the interview in Long Beach and relive the flight home. She really liked Michael, and she hoped he would call her.

*****

That same afternoon, Michael went shopping for a bed. He found a furniture store that was open and bought a king-sized bed with linens. The store promised to deliver it Monday afternoon. The air mattress he used the night before was uncomfortable, and since he didn't know when his furniture would get to his house, Michael thought the purchase of the bed seemed perfectly reasonable. He spent the rest of the day relaxing in a canvas chair on the deck looking at the lake.

The lawn between his house and the lake was expertly landscaped with flowering shrubs. His view of the lake was wide, showing the water that reflected the blue of the clear sky. It was beautiful and picturesque, but he saw none of it. Michael was deep in thought. He thought about the company and how he wanted to structure the personnel. He thought about changing the location of his manufacturing plants. But mostly, he thought about Angela Sutton.

CHAPTER 3

Monday morning, Michael drove to the new office in Huntersville. He opened the door to the lobby and walked inside. The lobby was light and airy with a wall of windows in the front. An attractive, professional looking receptionist, sat at the front desk. He approached her.

"Good morning. How can I help you?" she asked cheerfully with a friendly smile.

"Is the head of human resources in?" Michael asked.

The woman looked at her computer screen.

"He is," she answered. "Do you have an appointment?"

"Would you tell him that Michael Jamison is here and would like to speak with him?"

The woman started to pick up the phone, but

she looked at him and said, "Sir, I do believe you can just go on up."

Michael grinned, "Thank you."

He started to walk away, but turned, pointed to her and said, "Good job."

As Michael walked toward the elevator, the receptionist smiled and felt reassured that she was going to like working there.

Michael took the elevator to the third floor and walked down the hall to his office. He put his briefcase on his desk before walking down the stairs to the second floor. Human Resources, Information Technology, and Logistics shared that level.

Opening the door to the Human Resources Office, Michael walked in. George Martinez had been promoted to Director to oversee the moving of personnel to Charlotte. The large office was empty.

"George?" Michael called.

George came out of an office in the back of the room.

"Michael!" he exclaimed happily. "You made it."

Michael smiled and shook the man's hand.

"Did you get your family settled?" Michael asked.

"I did," George replied. "We found a place we like about twenty minutes from here, near Concord. How about you?"

"I'm still waiting on furniture," Michael groaned then asked, "Where are we on personnel? Who's moving here, where are they, and when will they get here?"

"As for managers, Dan in Logistics is here," George said. "Melissa in IT is here as well as Sheila in Product Development. You already know we're going to outsource legal services and accounting. We have a few other personnel who are working remotely while they make the transition to Charlotte. Everyone is beginning to trickle in, but they should all be here within the next two weeks."

"Good," Michael said. "As long as the work gets done, we can be understanding about working remotely. Who's here in Marketing?"

"Evie Barone is here. She was promoted to manager when Alex chose to retire instead of moving to Charlotte."

"Where are you on hiring the rest of the staff?" Michael asked.

"I have two interviews today for your administrative assistant. Do you want to be in the interviews?" George asked.

"I will if I'm free," Michael answered. "Email me the times and their applications. I can glance through them. What about the interviews you did in Long Beach? Any prospects?"

"Yes," George said. "But we're also interviewing here today, tomorrow, and Wednesday."

Michael nodded. "Would you call a staff meeting at ten this morning? Department heads only, and would you bring the applications for all the administrative positions."

Michael turned to leave then looked back at George and said, "I like the receptionist."

George smiled and watched his employer leave. He was just getting ready to go back to his office when Michael came back.

"Change of plans," Michael said. "Can I look through the applications now? I want to be familiar with who applied then hear why the managers do or do not want them." He smiled, "Don't worry, George. I'm not going to micromanage, but this is a new town and a completely different part of the country. There may be some differences between those of us from California and the residents here. I'm still trying to get used to the accent."

George laughed. "I understand completely."

*****

At ten o'clock, Michael started the meeting with the department managers. Everyone reported on the status of their departments, including which staff were moving and when they would arrive. Most of the staff had chosen to stay in California.

"Normally," Michael said, "I never micromanage, but this is a completely different set of circumstances. I've looked at the applications and notes that were made during the interviews. Who do you feel is best suited to be employed here?"

Each department head gave his or her recommendations for the applicants who had been interviewed. So far, Michael liked what he was hearing and felt that his managers were building good teams in their departments. Michael saved marketing for last.

"Evie, what about you?" he asked.

Evie Barone had dark brown eyes and short dark hair that framed her face in a flattering manner. Her professional business attire gave the impression of a competent manager.

"I had two interviews in Long Beach," she said, "and I have two tomorrow and Wednesday. They all look promising."

"Tell me about the ones in Long Beach,"

Michael said. "Are they willing to move to Char-lotte?"

"One is but he's totally unqualified. The other one is from here," Evie told him.

"Here?" Michael asked. He already knew the answer to the question, but he wanted to hear what Evie thought.

"She grew up near here and works for a food company in the eastern part of the state, but she only has a little over two years of experi-ence," Evie said dismissively.

"Why did she fly to Long Beach to inter-view when she could have interviewed here this week and saved the plane fare?" Michael asked.

"The applicant said that she has Fridays off if she works her hours in four days," Evie replied. "She chose to fly to California so she wouldn't have to take a day off to come to Charlotte in the middle of a work week. She looked at our interview appointments online and found one in California that matched her schedule."

"So, you're saying this applicant wanted a job with us badly enough to pay for an airline ticket and a hotel room because she didn't want to take a day away from her job?" Michael asked.

Evie shrugged, "That's what she said."

"That's commendable," Michael replied. "I

want that type of loyalty in an employee. I saw her application, and it looks like she has at least two years of experience in all the usual marketing tasks. There must be something that you didn't like, or you would be offering her a job."

Evie shrugged again, "I can't put my finger on it. I just don't think she'll fit in with the company."

Michael studied Evie intently. When she began to look nervous and broke eye contact, Michael decided she had something personal against Angela.

"I agree with Michael," George said. "An employee can learn tasks, but it's hard to learn a work ethic if you don't already have it by the time you finish college. I think we should hire her."

"I want to wait until the interviews are over, just in case someone better comes along," Evie said firmly.

"That's fair." George replied, noticing Evie's pursed lips and stoic expression. "I have them scheduled, but two have zero experience and want entry level. I don't recommend hiring them unless everyone else is completely unsuitable."

Evie looked at the table. Her face was flushed.

Her brow was furrowed, and she was clenching her jaw. Michael thought she looked angry. He would talk with George about the situation. Michael worried that Evie may not have been ready for the management position. The last thing he wanted was an inefficient manager who hired people because she was smarter than they were. He wanted good employees in place.

When the business was concluded, Michael adjourned the meeting but asked George to stay.

When everyone had left the room Michael asked George, "What's going on with Evie? She looked very uncomfortable with our desire to hire the woman from Durham."

"I noticed that, too," George replied, nodding in agreement. "I honestly think she's intimidated by the applicant. I was in her interview. The woman is bright and knowledgeable. She actually has more diverse marketing experience than Evie does. I would like to hire Ms. Sutton."

"I agree," Michael said. "On paper, she looks great. I want good people, but I also want cooperation among staff. Keep me informed about the other interviews and Evie's responses. I want to know if she's hiring inadequate people."

"I'll keep you posted," George said.

Michael looked at his watch.

"I need to leave," he said. "I have a delivery early this afternoon. If I don't come back, I'll be working from home, and you can reach me on my cellphone. I guess I won't be in those interviews. Both candidates have excellent resumes and qualifications. You decide. You did great with the receptionist."

*****

Evie Barone left the staff meeting with her jaws clenched so tightly it made her head hurt. She was annoyed and frustrated. Michael and George were insistent they hire that blond girl, the southern belle. Her accent had grated all over Evie's nerves.

"Well, I don't want her," Evie hissed aloud. She was too perfect on paper, too perfect in her presentation, and too perfect in her looks. How could she compete with Miss Too Perfect?

*****

Angela was covered in work. She had been out of the office early that morning for a meeting, and now she needed to send snack food orders to the processing plant for shipment. She began to check all her emails to make sure she had not missed any other orders.

However, as hard as Angela concentrated, the job at M & L Toys kept popping to the front of her mind, and Michael kept running in and out of her thoughts. He hadn't called her either of the two nights she had been home. She hoped he wasn't just playing her.

CHAPTER 4

On Monday afternoon, Michael's bed was delivered and assembled. He made the bed then checked his watch. It was three o'clock. If he left now, he could be in Durham in a little over two hours, or he could go back to the office.

Shaking his head, Michael took out his cellphone, looked through the contacts and called Angela's number. Honesty was important to Michael, and he needed to set the record straight with Angela about his owning M & L Toys. He could have done that with a phone call, but he wanted to see her.

Hearing her phone ring, Angela answered, "This is Angela."

"This is Michael," he said grinning.

Angela was glad she had a private office because she could not control the smile on her face or the sparkle in her eyes.

"Well, hello," Angela said, feeling butterflies in her stomach. "Are you in Charlotte or on the road?"

"Neither," Michael answered. "I'm actually at home, but I can get on the road and be in Durham shortly after five. Want to have dinner with me?"

"I would love to have dinner with you!" Angela exclaimed, beaming. "What type of food do you want?"

"You choose. I don't care," Michael said.

"Alright, there's a steak house a block from my office," Angela said. "I'll text you the name and address. Call me when you get there, and it will take me only five minutes to meet you."

"Perfect," Michael said. "I'll see you in a couple hours."

"I can't wait," Angela said. "See you soon."

Michael smiled and ended the call. He didn't bother to change clothes, and five minutes later, he was driving down the highway to the interstate that would take him to Durham.

*****

Angela couldn't believe that Michael had called and that he wanted to have dinner with her. She was going to have to be careful. It wouldn't take her long to develop feelings for him.

Shortly before six, Angela's cell phone rang.

"Hey Michael," she said.

"I'm at the restaurant," he said. "I'll get us a table."

"I'll be right there," Angela replied.

Smiling, Angela hurried to the bathroom to check her hair and makeup then practically ran to her car. Five minutes later, she parked in front of the restaurant. She paused at the door, took a deep breath and walked inside.

"Just one?" the hostess asked.

"I'm meeting a friend. He should've just come inside," Angela replied.

"I think your friend is over here," the hostess said, pointing to the right.

She led Angela to where Michael was sitting and looking at a menu. Angela felt butterflies in her stomach again. She was so glad to see him. Angela thanked the hostess and sat down opposite Michael in the booth.

Michael looked up to see Angela walking toward him. He was sure his heart skipped a beat. She wore a navy blue business suit and had pulled her hair back in a smooth ponytail. The woman whom he had thought of as attractive was actually beautiful.

"Hello," Michael said smiling as he stood to greet her.

Angela settled in her seat. She looked at him and smiled.

"Hello," she said. "How was the drive?"

"I couldn't tell if this was North Carolina or California. Traffic was heavy, but it was worth it to be here having dinner with you," he replied.

"And I'm happy you braved the horrible NC traffic. Really, it's so good to see you," she said, unable to stop her wide smile.

The waitress came to take their orders. After the couple told her what they wanted, the waitress took the menus and left.

"You look very professional," Michael said. "I don't know why I thought that being with a small company you would be business casual."

"I am, usually," Angela answered. "I had a morning appointment with the buyer for a small grocery chain in the eastern part of the state."

"Did you make the sale?" he asked.

"I did. That man sampled everything I brought him. He placed a significant order and requested we keep his stores stocked with our product. I was ecstatic," Angela said with a wide smile.

"I'm sure you were," Michael said, smiling back at her.

"Tell me about your place in Charlotte," Angela said. "Did you get your furniture?"

Michael paused when the waitress brought their food then shook his head.

"My furniture is somewhere between California and Charlotte," he said. "I went into town yesterday afternoon and bought a bed. My back let me know that it doesn't like sleeping on an air mattress."

Angela nodded in agreement, "I used to sleep on them all the time as a kid, but I agree. I don't think I would enjoy that now."

"I bought a house on Lake Norman. The view is pretty awesome," he said with a mischievious grin.

Angela laughed, "Then why did you let me go on about the best places to go boating or fishing?"

"I just wanted to hear what you had to say," Michael replied.

"Humph," Angela said, squinting at him. "You're a stinker."

Michael laughed, "A stinker? I've never been called a stinker. This is a first."

"Hey, if the shoe fits!" Angela said with a

straight face and shrugging.

Michael laughed, and the two continued to talk through dinner, getting to know each other better. The waitress took their plates, and Michael ordered the death by chocolate and two spoons.

When the dessert arrived, he looked at Angela. "I owe you an apology."

"Why?" Angela asked incredulously.

"On the plane when you told me you had interviewed with M & L Toys, I should have told you that I'm employed by them," he said. "That's why I moved to Charlotte. I just wanted to hear about your experience in Long Beach."

Angela took a bite of the dessert, leaned back in her seat, looked at him and crossed her arms.

"Oh my gosh. You're the Michael Jamison who owns the company," she said, blushing slightly with embarrassment.

Michael winced, "Guilty. Please don't be mad. When you told me you had interviewed with M & L Toys, I decided I wanted to get to know you before you found out my status in the company. I came to not only take you to dinner, but I wanted to clear the air. Honesty is important, and I respect you enough that I didn't want to be deceitful."

"Well, I should be angry with you, but I'm not," she reassured him. "I probably would have made a fool of myself if I had known. I would've been giddy trying to impress you, or tongue-tied in discomfort.

Michael laughed. "So, I'm forgiven?"

"Sure. I don't hold grudges." Angela gave him the same squinty look she had given him on the plane. She pointed her spoon at him and said, "But you forfeit your half of the dessert."

Michael burst into laughter. "I can deal with that as long as you aren't mad at me."

"Well, I'm glad you came, and I'm glad you told me the truth," she said. "If I happened to get the job and stood in shock the first time I saw you in the halls, I might not have handled it so genteelly."

"Genteelly?" Michael asked, raising an eyebrow inquisitively.

"Yes. We southern women are always calm and genteel," she said then rolled her eyes. "Believe that and I'll sell you some swamp land down east."

"Swamp land?" Michael asked grinning. "I can honestly say I've never seen a swamp."

"You're not missing anything," Angela said emphatically. "They're wet and full of snakes and mosquitoes. I stay away from them."

Michael laughed.

Angela paused for a moment. "Are you going to break it to me gently that I didn't get the job? I mean, if I were employed, we probably violated some sort of company policy about employees seeing each other outside the office."

"No. I came to see you because I wanted to," he reassured her. "They haven't finished interviewing for the positions in that department."

"But enough about the company," Michael said, abruptly changing the subject. "Where did you go to college?"

"I went to NC State University in Raleigh," Angela said. "My dad went there, so it was a no brainer that I attend. I enjoyed it. How about you?"

"UCLA. The uncles went there, so it was a no brainer that I attend," he said smiling.

"Uncles?" Angela asked.

"Max and Louis Niche. They started M & L Toys," Michael told her. "Mom married and had me. Then, Dad left. She struggled as a single parent, so the uncles moved us in with them and hired her to do the bookkeeping for the company. No one had any idea it would be so successful. The uncles never married. They were obsessed with toys, and they loved me."

"Who do you look like?" Angela asked.

"The uncles," he replied. "Mom looks like them, too. It's a Mediterranean heritage."

"As you can see, I have a northern European heritage. I'm a walking sunburn," she said.

After a few more minutes of talking, Michael looked around the restaurant.

"I imagine the waitress would like us to go so she can turn the table over to more customers," he said. "Is there anywhere we can go to talk?"

Angela gave him that intense squinty look that she has when she's thinking. He grinned.

"Yes," she said. "Follow me."

Michael paid the check, then he and Angela walked to their cars. Michael followed her through some back streets to a condominium complex. She parked, and he parked beside her.

When they were on the sidewalk, Angela said, "This will be the most comfortable place. I decided you weren't a serial killer."

Michael laughed. "No, I'm not that. Is this your place?"

"Yes," Angela said as she punched some buttons on the security panel outside the main door.

"Nice," Michael said as he heard the door unlock. "That security door must be reassuring."

"It is until you have to go in and out multiple times, but it's still worth it." Angela led him down the hall and unlocked a door. "Welcome to my space."

Michael looked around. There were two bedrooms, a living area, kitchen, and dining area. The place was neat and decorated in cool colors with a mixture of modern and rustic furniture. Several pieces of colorful art hung on the walls, revealing another side to Angela's bright personality.

"Have a seat," Angela said as she pointed to the couch. "Would you like something to drink?"

"Do you have any coffee?" he asked. "I may need the caffeine to get back to Charlotte."

"Do you need to leave now?" she asked.

Michael shook his head, "No, I'll stay till you throw me out. You're my only friend on this side of the country." He winked.

"Poor you," Angela said grinning. "You must be desperate for a friend if that's true. Cream or sugar?"

"Black," Michael said.

Angela brought him the coffee and sat beside him on the couch. Angela and Michael resumed their conversation, discovering things they had in common. They lost track of time until Michael looked out the window and saw that it was completely dark.

Seeing that it was getting late, Michael stood and said, "I'd better go. It'll be midnight when I get home, and you need to get some rest, too."

"I'm so glad you came," Angela said as she stood. "I have thoroughly enjoyed spending time with you. I'm going home this weekend. Maybe we can hang out closer to your place."

"I'd like that," Michael said. "Thank you for a wonderful evening, Angela."

Angela nodded. Their eyes locked and lingered for a few seconds before Michael turned to leave. She watched him walk down the hall and out the security door. She wished Michael had kissed her, but decided it was best that he hadn't, at least not until she got the letter stating she hadn't been hired.

Michael got in his car and started the drive home. He was in trouble. He had wanted to kiss Angela. It had taken every ounce of self-control he had to not do so. He needed to wait and see if George and Evie decided to hire her. The last thing he wanted was awkwardness in the workplace.

CHAPTER 5

Max Niche looked at his brother, Louis, and said, "I can't believe we weren't able to change Michael's mind about moving the business out of California."

"As much as I hate to say this, but maybe we should move to Charlotte as well," Louis said.

"Do you really think that's necessary?" Max asked.

"Yes," Louis said, nodding. "Our day of reckoning is not far away. I'm hoping that passing the company along to Michael will protect it. We're the ones who made the bargain, not Michael."

"Charlotte seems so far away," Max said. "Will Eleanor want to go, too?"

"Of course," Louis replied. "She's his mother, but she has no idea what we did. Besides, Eleanor is a prayer warrior in her faith. I'm sure she's the reason Michael hasn't been approached by one of Baal's representatives. I'm also convinced that Eleanor is the reason we haven't been bothered for so long. Her prayers of protection keep Baal out of this house and our minds. We need her."

"Do you think Baal knows what we did and that Michael has moved the company?" Max asked.

"I don't know," Louis answered. "Baal isn't omnipotent. He doesn't know everything. He relies on his tattling minions to let him know what's happening everywhere." Louis stood, "Why don't you start looking at real estate near Charlotte. I'll go talk with Eleanor."

*****

Louis walked into the den to find Eleanor sitting on the couch. His sister was a very attractive woman. She was petite with dark hair, brown eyes, and an olive complexion. At first Louis thought she was just sitting and staring into space, but then he realized she was praying.

Eleanor turned to him and said, "We need to move to Charlotte, Louis. I need to protect Michael."

"How do you know?" Louis asked with a

shocked expression. It was if she could read his mind.

Eleanor looked at him.

"I'm not stupid, Louis. I know the bargain you and Max made for success and riches. You sold your souls to the devil himself," she said, sarcastically blunt. "The only thing that has kept your mistake from harming Michael is the cover of prayer. You tell your master that I took Michael to church. He accepted Jesus and was baptized. Baal can't have Michael."

"I should have taken him from here when he was a boy," she continued, sounding both sad and annoyed. "But you and Max have been good role models for him regardless of your decision.

Louis sighed, "You're right, Eleanor. Max and I made a terrible mistake all those years ago. We were young and stupid, eager and impatient. Max is already looking at real estate in the Charlotte area. Why don't you come into the office, and we can all look at the properties for sale."

Eleanor nodded and followed her brother. The three siblings scrolled through the listings. Their plan was to rent a house in Huntersville until they found a place to buy. They felt the need to get to Charlotte as quickly as posible to support Michael. After finding a few properties they would like to look at, Eleanor left the room to pack.

*****

While driving home from Durham, Michael's phone rang. He looked at the ID and pushed the accept button.

"Hello, Mom. How are you?" he asked.

"I'm fine," Eleanor replied. "Are you driving?"

"Yes. I'm driving back from Durham," he answered.

"But it's so late. I almost didn't call," she said.

"I'm glad you did," he replied. "You can talk to me and keep me awake. How are the uncles?"

"That's why I'm calling," she said. "I'm letting you know that the three of us miss you, and we want to be closer to you. So, we decided to move to the Charlotte area, too. We're going to rent a house while we look for a property to buy, and we're flying there tomorrow."

"That's great news! I was starting to miss my family, and I've only been here three days," he said laughing. "I would invite you to stay with me, but my furniture hasn't arrived from Long Beach, and my house is too small. It only has one extra bedroom. What type of property do you want?"

"We want a house big enough for the three of us," she said. "We found a few for sale that might work well. We thought about downsizing, but to get three bedrooms with their own baths may be difficult without getting a large house."

"I'm sure you'll find what you're looking for," he said.

"Why were you in Durham?" Eleanor asked.

"I had dinner with a friend," he answered. "We talked a long time, and now I'm paying the late night price, but I'm not sorry."

"I didn't think you knew anyone there," Eleanor said.

"I didn't. We met on the flight and talked all the way to Charlotte. Her name is Angela," he said grinning.

"Oh, you met a woman you like?" Eleanor asked.

"Yes. I like her very much," he replied. "Unfortunately, she has applied for a job with the company. That's why she was in Long Beach. She had an interview."

"Did she get the job?" Eleanor asked.

"They're still interviewing applicants," Michael told her. "I'm staying out of it. I can't be accused of favoritism. I'm almost hoping they don't offer her a job, but she's qualified."

"You sound serious. Isn't it a little soon?" she asked.

"I can't explain it, Mom. Everything is so easy with her, and she's beautiful. I've dated beautiful women, but Angela's different. It's like an inner beauty spilling over to the outside."

"I would like to meet the woman who finally captured my son's attention. Is she a Christian?" Eleanor asked.

"Honestly, we didn't talk about that," Michael said.

"That's very important, Michael. Find out soon. Don't let your heart get attached to an unequally yoked relationship," Eleanor warned.

Michael started to get irritated with Eleanor then remembered she just had his best interest at heart.

"Mom, I understand," he said patiently. "You have preached about the yoked relationship since I was thirteen. Give me credit for being able to make a wise decision."

"You're right, Michael," Eleanor replied. "You're an adult and quite capable of making good decisions, but you're also capable of making unwise decisions like the rest of us. I will pray that you make the right one and drop the subject."

"Thank you, Mom. I always appreciate your prayers," he said with affection. "I just turned into my driveway, so I'm going to go inside and get some sleep. Tomorrow is a busy day. Moving an entire company across the country comes with some unique problems, but I'm glad we're doing this. You'll like it here."

"Of course I'll like it," she said. "I'll be closer to my favorite son! Goodnight, Michael."

"Night, Mom," Michael said and ended the call.

Knowing his family was moving to the area gave him a sense of peace that only family living nearby could give. Michael parked, closed the garage and went inside. He fell asleep smiling and thinking about Angela.

CHAPTER 6

Michael yawned as he came through the front door of the M & L Toys building.

He heard a cheerful, "Good morning, Mr. Jamison."

The workspace for the receptionist was long, narrow and at bar height. She was sitting in a very comfortable chair that was ergonomically correct for working there. Michael walked over and put his briefcase on the counter. When he looked at her, the woman was smiling.

"Millie," Michael said, "two things. First, I want you to call me Michael. Everyone else in the building does." Michael propped his elbow on the desk and leaned his head into his fist, "Second, is there coffee anywhere in this building?"

Millie laughed and said, "Mr. Jamison, I mean, Michael, follow me."

Millie led Michael to a room behind her desk. It was a very comfortable looking lounge with a refrigerator, microwave, sink, tables and chairs. On the counter was a pot of hot coffee.

She pointed to the coffee and said, "Disposable cups and sugar are in the cabinet. Creamer is in the refrigerator."

"Millie," Michael said, "at this moment in time, you are my most favorite person in the world. Thank you." He walked over and poured a cup of coffee.

The phone rang, and Millie left to answer it. Michael walked back through the lobby and took the elevator to the third floor. Normally he would take the stairs, but this morning he was just too tired.

The caffeine began to wake him up, and Michael sat at his desk reading the latest production and sales reports. He looked up when he heard a knock at his door.

"Come in, George," Michael said and gestured to the seat in front of his desk.

"You look tired," George said.

Michael yawned and nodded.

"My mother called," he said. "I think she forgot there's a three hour time difference between here and California."

"How is Eleanor?" George asked.

"Good, but she and the uncles feel like empty nesters. They're moving here, too," Michael said smiling.

George laughed, "I wondered how long it would take Max and Louis to do that. This company may be yours now, but it's their baby."

"Yes," Michael said smiling. "It'll be good to have them here. What do you need?"

"This is your new administrative assistant," George said as he handed Michael a folder.

Michael opened the file. "Helen Stinson. A retired teacher?"

George nodded, "She's the best candidate. She taught business classes at both a high school and a community college. Also, she's Millie Taylor's best friend. I talked to Millie, and she highly recommended Helen."

"When does she start?" Michael asked.

"Monday," George answered. "She'll be starting along with one or two in each department except marketing. I'll do a one-day orientation then send them to their immediate boss. You should expect her sometime after lunch."

"Well, Millie's an asset, that's for sure," Michael said. "I can only guess that Helen will be, too. Thanks. Why does marketing not have anyone starting?"

"Evie doesn't want to make a decision until everyone is interviewed. Plus, the ones with the most potential are employed and will need to give notice," George replied.

"Sounds reasonable," Michael said, "but she can't run that department alone. I hate that none of the experienced marketing staff chose to move to Charlotte. Don't let her wait past tomorrow to hire someone. She needs help."

"I agree," George said. "If she won't make the decision, I will decide by tomorrow evening." He paused, "Michael, I'm worried that Evie may be in over her head as manager of the department. She does a great job when you give her a task, but she's having trouble making decisions."

Michael looked thoughtful then said, "Let's gently lead her along until she learns and becomes comfortable managing a department. She's loyal enough to move across the country. I would hate for her to do that only to lose her job."

"Agreed," George said. "I'll keep an eye on her." He got up to leave. "I'll be out of the office part of tomorrow. Construction is just about finished at the electronic toy factory. Peter and I are holding a job fair for anyone who wants to apply. Some of those positions are just above minimum wage to start, and none of those California employees chose to move."

"Good," Michael said. "As soon as it's up and running, we'll shut the California plant down and sell the building. My realtor has a buyer for the building and the equipment, but I want to check with Peter about that since he's the manager for all the electronic merchandise. I'm not inclined to sell the equipment and give another company a foothold in this business. It's competitive enough as it is."

As George left the office, Michael thought about Peter. He and Peter Newland had been best friends since meeting their freshman year at UCLA. Peter was an electrical engineer and had become a valued member of the company. Then Michael's thoughts turned to Angela. He really wanted to see her again, so he took out his phone and texted her.

Michael: Good morning. Enjoyed last night. Very sleepy this morning, but the evening was worth it.

Angela: Glad you got home safely. I enjoyed the evening, too.

Michael: Still coming this weekend?

Angela: For sure. Weather looks good. Helping

Dad Friday and Saturday.

Michael: What's he doing?

Angela: Harvesting wheat. Forgot to tell you, I grew up on a farm.

Michael: Awesome. Save some time somewhere to hang out. You know your schedule, let me know what works for you.

Angela: Alright. Probably Saturday. We will work well into the evening Friday.

Michael: Sounds good. Talk soon.

*****

Eleanor, Max, and Louis boarded their connection in Salt Lake City. Their flight would land in Charlotte late in the afternoon eastern time. They all sat together in a row with three seats.

Halfway to Charlotte, Max and Louis fell asleep, and Eleanor was reading. Suddenly the air around the seats beside her felt cold, and the lights appeared to dim. She looked around the plane. No one seemed to be experiencing the same thing. Eleanor shivered as the strange cold kept creeping in, like a sudden drop in temperature that was only happening at their seats.

While Eleanor had never witnessed anything

Max and Louis did or experienced since getting involved with Baal, she was sure a demon was nearby, possibly entering her brothers' dreams. She looked at the two men. Their eyes were open, and they looked as if they were in a deep trance. Eleanor leaned over her tray table and turned her head toward her brothers.

She whispered, "In the name of Jesus Christ, I command the demons of Satan to leave. You have no authority here. Leave this place. Jesus is Lord and he is victorious over death and sin. He is victorious over you." Eleanor whispered those words over and over.

*****

Max and Louis had been reading when they became very drowsy and fell asleep. They both began to dream. When the two realized that they were together, they knew this was more than a mere dream. Wherever they were, there was fog everywhere. It was a thick grey fog, more like toxic smoke than a mist. Fear set in as the fog enveloped them. They couldn't see anything around them except each other. Then the temperature dropped to a cold that chilled them to their core.

Max and Louis looked at each other, anxiety growing in their chests. He knew. Baal knew what they had done, and he was coming to punish them at best. At worst, they would die. The fog began to move.

Out of the grey mist walked Baal. Max and Louis watched Baal as he approached them. Their fear was so great they could barely breathe. All they could do was watch because as hard as they tried, they couldn't move. Baal had done something to paralyze them in place.

Baal was tall, muscular, and handsome. But as he got closer, the brothers could see the evil in his black eyes and his snarling grin.

Max and Louis had personally encountered Baal only the few times he appeared at the monthly ceremony while everyone was in a trance. Each time, he always looked slightly different. Sometimes he liked wearing the clothes of a Roman gladiator or soldier. At other times he wore the long flowing robes associated with spirits and angels. Today, Baal was dressed in a designer business suit. Being dramatic was a favorite action of his as well, which he demonstrated as he slowly walked around Max and Louis.

"Hello, Max. Hello, Louis," he said softly but ominously, his voice deep and threatening. "Do you know why I'm here?"

Neither Max nor Louis could move or talk. Frozen in place, they felt tears running down their cheeks as they awaited their fate. Regret for giving into the temptation for money and success and for signing that contract was almost as palpable as their fear.

"Oh, can't speak?" Baal asked sarcastically. "Too bad. I will tell you. I am very unhappy with you boys. Do you know why?"

Baal stood in front of them and suddenly projected the image of a gruesome, horned face that was half human, half bull. His eyes were yellow with black slits for pupils, and black wings, much like those of a bat, extended from his back. Baal's exposed chest and arms had black and gray scales like a snake, and a foul smelling spittle drained from his mouth like drool. Max and Louis realized with horror that they could not close their eyes against the hideous form Baal chose to present to them.

Raising his hands, which looked like the knarled talons of a vulture, Baal grabbed the brothers by their necks and squeezed. He lifted them above the ground, causing more stress on their throats. Max and Louis couldn't breathe, and they couldn't move to try and get away. Intense fear made their hearts race, and they felt warm urine soaking their clothes.

Just as Max and Louis were about to pass out, knowing they were going to die, Baal screamed, "You gave my toy company away!"

Baal released them with a shove. Max and Louis fell to the ground, unable to stand. They laid there, still unable to move, and looked up at Baal. Just as suddenly, Baal returned to his original form. He reached down and pulled Max and Louis up to a standing position.

Letting go of the two men, Baal calmly said, "I am very angry about that. You gave my toy company to a filthy Christian! That's what makes me so mad." Baal looked them in the eye and said, "I want it back."

Suddenly, Baal turned pale and stumbled. His breath caught in his chest as he looked beside Max and Louis and saw Eleanor praying.

Baal screamed, "I want that company back, and get rid of that praying woman!"

Max and Louis watched as Baal grew weak and fled. They were suddenly able to move, then they were awake, still on the plane. The brothers looked at each other, coughing, and gasping for air. They each had reddened necks and pin pricks of blood showed on their collars.

The two rubbed their throats and looked at

each other with the worst fear they had ever felt. The stench of Baal's drool lingered in the air around their seats, but their clothes were dry. Baal must have been taken by surprise, and the urine on their clothes had been a dream, not real. Unfortunately, the blood on their necks was very real.

Louis, who was in the middle, touched Eleanor's shoulder. She stopped praying and looked at her brothers, noticing the temperature had returned to normal.

"Are you alright?" she asked. Eleanor could see the fear on their faces and even feel it emanating from them. "I know that monster was here." She saw their necks. "What happened, and what's that smell?"

"Yes, he was here." Louis looked at Eleanor and said, "He tried to choke us to make a point. That smell is his breath. We watched him grow weak and run away before he could hurt us more. He yelled at us to get the company back and to get rid of the praying woman. Eleanor, you are a strong warrior. He's afraid of you. I'm in awe. Thank you."

Eleanor looked at them both with surprise. Max nodded in agreement. Eleanor gave a weak smile and put her head back against her seat. It was apparent that Baal was angry that her brothers had turned the company over to Michael. She was also sure that a spiritual war had begun.

Eleanor took a deep breath and softly said, "Prayer 1, Baal 0," and fell asleep.

"What do we do?" Max asked as he rubbed his neck. "I've never been so afraid or so humiliated in my entire life."

"I have no idea," Louis replied, "but I will do everything I can to protect Michael and that company. We need to protect Eleanor, too. She can keep Baal away, but that won't stop him from trying to eliminate her. He could very easily arrange for an accident of some kind."

Still shaking from the experience, the brothers sat back in their seats. They rubbed their sore necks and were frighteningly aware that they could still smell the spittle from Baal's mouth.

*****

After the plane landed in Charlotte, the three siblings deboarded and collected their luggage. Their car had been reserved, and they soon arrived at their rental house. Once they had everything unloaded, Eleanor called Michael.

"Mom!" he said happily. "Are you in Charlotte?"

"Yes, Dear," she answered. "We're here. Our rental house is in the Huntersville area not too far from your office. Would you like to have dinner with us?"

"Of course," Michael answered. "Where do you want to go?"

"We saw a nice little Italian bistro just off the interstate at the exit south of where your building is. Would you like to meet us there at six?"

"Yes. I know the place you're talking about. I'll see you at six," he said, and they ended the call.

After work, Michael went to the restaurant and ate dinner with his family. While enjoying the Italian food, Michael shared information about moving the company, having to hire so many new employees, and keeping production going for the Christmas season. Max and Louis encouraged him but only after teasing him about overthinking the process. When they were leaving the restaurant, Eleanor gave him a piece of paper with their address.

"We have an appointment in the morning with a realtor, but we won't be looking at houses all day," she said. "Come have dinner with us."

"I would love to," Michael said. "I'll call you when I leave the office."

Michael kissed his mother on the cheek and hugged his uncles. He told them good night and expressed how happy he was that they were moving to the area. Michael drove home feeling almost as good as he had when he left Durham the night before.

CHAPTER 7

T hursday morning, Angela sat at her desk, engrossed in her work. Her phone rang.

She absently answered, "This is Angela."

"Angela Sutton, this is George Martinez with the M & L Toy Company." Shocked, Angela stopped what she was doing.

"Hello, Mr. Martinez. How are you today?" she asked.

George smiled and replied, "I'm fine, thank you for asking. I called to offer you a job with our company."

Surprised and excited, Angela listened as George outlined her primary duties and quoted her a salary that surprised her. She had no idea she would get that large of a raise in pay for a new job.

After giving Angela the details, George asked,

"Will you accept the job?"

Angela felt butterflies in her stomach.

She took a deep breath and said, "Thank you, Mr. Martinez. I accept the position. I'm really looking forward to working with your company."

"That's great. When can you start?" he asked.

"Can I call you right back?" she asked. "I assume two weeks, but I'd like to discuss that with my current employer."

"I understand," George said. "You have my number, so feel free to call me anytime this week."

"Thank you, Mr. Martinez. I appreciate the opportunity you're giving me," Angela said.

"You're welcome. We're glad to have you joining our team," George said and ended the call.

Angela took another deep breath. Her nerves were a mess, but she couldn't keep from smiling. Now, she just had to break the news to her boss, which wouldn't be easy due to the amount of respect she had for him.

Angela walked down the hall to her employer's office. More butterflies filled her stomach as she knocked on the door.

"Mr. Thomas, may I speak with you please?" Angela asked.

James Thomas looked up and smiled. "Sure, Angela. What's on your mind?"

Angela sat in the chair in front of the man's desk.

"I've been offered a job in the marketing department with the M & L Toy Company, and I accepted," she told him. "It wasn't an easy decision because I've really enjoyed this job, and I appreciate the opportunity you gave me when you hired me. But this move will also let me move back home to the farm. I just wanted to tell you in person and see how long of a notice you want me to work."

"This is crazy!" James he said as looked at Angela.

"What?" she asked, concerned.

"Angela, one of my good friends has a son who just graduated from college with a marketing degree. He can't find a job anywhere. They asked me if I had an opening, and I said no. That was last week. Don't get me wrong, Angela, I hate to lose you. You're one of the best people we've had in that position since I took over the company, but to be able to offer an entry level job to a young man to help a friend is amazing. Could you work next week and orient him? Then you're free to start your new job whenever you choose."

Angela smiled, "I will be happy to work with your new graduate, and I'm glad things are working out in such a way that we can all feel good about it."

James nodded. He stood and shook Angela's hand.

"Congratulations, Angela. You'll have more opportunities for advancement there than you would here. I'm happy for you," he said with genuine warmth.

"Thank you, Mr. Thomas. I'll try to not leave any loose ends," Angela said.

"I never thought you would, Angela," he replied. Angela smiled and left his office feeling a massive sense of relief.

Back in her office, Angela called George to let him know she would work a one week notice and could start any time after next Friday. They agreed that she would start the following Monday. Once all the arrangements were made, Angela ended the call, excited for the upcoming change in her life. For the rest of the day, she focused on her job and what she needed to do before she left the position.

*****

That afternoon, Michael heard a knock on his office door. He looked up to see George.

"Hey, come in," he said.

George approached Michael's desk and handed him a list of new employees, their departments, and their start dates.

"It looks like you're going to have several large orientations over the next few weeks," Michael said.

"I think we have a good group of new hires starting, and we're still interviewing," George said.

Michael looked at the list, "You only have one employee starting in marketing in the next three weeks. Why?"

"Evie is still pondering," George said, sounding frustrated. "I called Angela Sutton myself. When I told Evie that I hired Angela, she got very defensive. I explained to Evie that we had to get staff hired and not wait so long to make the decision."

George paused then said, "I don't know what Evie has against the woman, but I think Ms. Sutton will be an asset. She's a one man show where she is now which means she has done everything from direct sales to ads." He paused then continued, "Ms. Sutton is a lot more versatile than the manager in the department. That could end up being a problem. I'll keep my eye on things. I don't want to lose a good employee because the manager resents her for some unknown reason."

Michael nodded. "Thanks. I agree with you on that."

*****

Angela worked her fortieth hour for the week. Before she left, she created an agenda for the next week's orientation of the new marketing employee. She drove to her condo where her suitcase was already packed.

After changing clothes Angela took the opportunity to fill a storage bin with winter clothes, excited to start the moving process. She couldn't wait to tell her parents she was moving back home.

*****

It was after eight o'clock, and Angela still had another hour of driving ahead of her. Fatigue from the week was settling in. She took a sip of the caffeinated drink in her cup holder, hoping it would help.

The sound of her phone ringing startled her. Looking at the electronic screen on her SUV dashboard, Angela smiled. She pushed the button for accept.

"Hello, Michael," she said. "Did you have a good day?"

Michael smiled, "I did. I hope you did as well."

"Mine was exciting," Angela said cryptically.

"Oh? How was it exciting?" he asked.

"I got really nervous when I had to tell my boss I had taken another job," Angela said.

"How did that go?" he asked seriously.

"Well, it turns out that my leaving helps the son of my employer's good friend get an entry level job. I orient him next week and start the following week at M & L," she said.

"How do you feel about working at my company?" Michael asked.

"That was my goal before I met you, so I've accomplished that. Michael, I really want to work there, but I also don't want it to make our friendship awkward," Angela replied.

"I think we can be professional on the job and friends off the job. There are several employees who are friends after hours. We probably won't see each other during the day, anyway, so don't worry." Michael paused then asked, "So when and where are we hanging out this weekend?"

"I'm not sure yet. I'll know tomorrow night. We'll be up before the sun comes up and quit after the sun goes down," she said.

"That's a very long day. Do you get paid for that?" he asked.

"No. It's a family farm," Angela replied. "We all work together. I may not get cash, but there are other benefits like the satisfaction of helping my dad with the work and fresh food from the garden. Then there's Blazer."

"Who's Blazer?" Michael asked.

"My horse. We have a mutual admiration society. I think the other horses get jealous," she said laughing.

"You have horses?" he asked.

"Yes," she replied. "Do you ride?"

"Not in a while," he answered.

"We'll have to do that," she said. "We own three hundred acres and rent another four hundred acres from nearby landowners. That gives us a lot of trails to ride on. The neighbors are used to seeing me checking the crops on horseback."

"Wow, that's a lot of acres. All the land I own is around my house. I would love to go riding with you sometime." Michael continued, "I was notified that my furniture arrives Saturday. Maybe I'll have things set up enough that we can hang out on the deck."

"That would be fun," she said. "We have a pond, but there's nothing like the view of the lake."

"I agree." Michael paused then said, "I'm really glad you're coming to work for us. You have a diverse skill set on your application."

Angela laughed, "I ran out of room. I just wrote what I did most."

"But I'm also glad I get to see you every day when I'm in town," he said.

"I'm happy about that, too," Angela said. "You're turning into my best friend. I would rather hang out with you than my female friends."

"Well, you're still my only friend," Michael said wryly.

Angela laughed. "Oh, poor you."

"I forgot to tell you, my mother and the uncles are in town. They've decided to move here, too." Michael said in a confident voice, "I think they missed me."

"I'm sure, but I also think you missed them," Angela said with a knowing tone in her voice.

"You're right, I did," Michael answered.

After more bantering, Angela said, "Well, I'm home. I'll talk with you tomorrow or Saturday."

"Alright. Glad you made it safely," Michael said and ended the call. He stared at his phone, aware of his growing feelings for Angela. It was both exciting and a little scary at just how fast those feelings had developed. Pondering the conversation, he smiled. Evidently Angela had growing feelings, too.

CHAPTER 8

It was Friday morning, and Michael looked at his watch for the fifth time in as many minutes. Thank goodness he had a meeting with the product development team at nine. He needed to concentrate and focus, but all his mind wanted to do was think about Angela and the fact that she was so close.

He shook his head and scolded himself. Picking up his laptop and a legal pad, Michael took the stairs to the first floor. The lobby was small. Except for the nice-sized employee lounge and a small gym, the entire floor was devoted to product research and development. He was getting ready to hear ideas about new toys being developed and ways to compete with the latest hot new toys that weren't theirs.

Two hours later, Michael was back in his office. He was pleased with the work of the department. They were in good shape for the competitive holidays this year and next year.

Hoping Angela had taken a lunch break, he texted her.

Michael: Hey, how's the harvest going?

There was no immediate return text. Instead, his phone rang. It was Angela.

"Hey," he said. "How's the harvest going?"

"Good," Angela answered, "but I can't text. I keep both hands on the steering wheel and eyes on the combine. This is a large seven-ton truck, but a collision with a larger combine would cause extreme damage on both."

"You drive equipment that big?" he asked. "I'm impressed."

"There are bigger combines and bigger trucks out there, but our fields aren't large enough to need them," she said. "We're about halfway through all the fields. We're filling the big truck for Mom to take to the mill this afternoon. Dad has a contract to fulfill. The rest will go into the grain bins until he's ready to sell it. Mom and Dad had started the harvest a couple days ago, but with the three of us working, it'll go a lot faster."

Michael heard a male voice on a radio saying, "Brake hard."

Angela answered, "Copy. I'll go check."

"Michael, I have to go. A doe just jumped up and ran. We need to make sure there isn't a fawn in the way. We don't like hurting the wildlife. I'll call you later," she said and ended the call.

Angela put the truck in park, got out and walked the rows of wheat ahead of the combine. About thirty feet in front of them was a fawn. It jumped up on wobbly legs and ran after its mother.

Angela and Ray resumed their work, and at the end of the row, she saw the doe standing beside the fawn. Angela smiled.

Michael didn't hear from Angela again until it was dark. She texted him.

Angela: Long day. If we don't finish tomorrow, Mom and Dad can finish next week. Need shower and fluids. Old truck doesn't have air conditioner like the big one.

Michael: That's tough. It was hot this afternoon.

Angela: It's been hotter. Wish we could have spent time together today, maybe tomorrow. You're getting your furniture tomorrow. You may not have time.

Michael: Oh, I will find the time.

Angela: OK. My time will depend on Dad. I'll keep you posted. Talk to you tomorrow.

Michael: Rest well.

*****

That evening, Eleanor, Max, and Louis sat around the table of their rental house eating take-out from a local restaurant. They were tired.

"We looked at eight properties in two days," Max said. "I would've been happy with just five of them. Three were an absolute no."

"I liked the third one," Eleanor said. "I liked the layout, the color scheme, and the fact that it's on Lake Norman. Nice deck, nice view."

"I did too," Louis said. "Max?"

"I can live with number three. Let's get that one," Max replied.

Louis said, "Alright. I'll call the realtor and make an offer tomorrow. Let's sleep on it and discuss it one more time in the morning." They nodded in agreement before retiring to their rooms for the night.

*****

Over the centuries, Baal had moved his primary center of operation from Babylon to Rome and finally to Washington, DC. This is where the challenge was. His goal was to remove Christianity from the whole country. He was still angry about his meeting with Max and Louis. That praying woman had made him look weak in front of his two recruits. He thought she might be the reason they gave the company away. If Max and Louis started regretting their choices, she could tell them about the only way they could get out of the contract, and he couldn't risk that.

Xada, his second in command, was standing nearby. While Baal liked changing his looks, Xada never wavered in appearance. He was blond, strong, and handsome from a distance; however, on closer inspection, the evil in his black eyes made even the strongest of the demons frightened. Xada consistently wore a type of dark gray, loose battle clothing. Baal never got his hands dirty in a battle, but Xada did. He was a powerful warrior for the fallen angels that made up Baal's army.

Baal motioned Xada over and said, "M & L Toys has been given to a Christian."

"I heard," Xada said.

"The new owner's mother is a praying woman," Baal said, sounding disgusted. "Neutralize her. I don't want her to influence those brothers to get out of their contract. There's only one way they can do that, and I don't want her giving them any ideas."

"How do you want this done?" Xada asked.

"I don't care." Baal paused then said, "Let's have some fun. Don't kill her. Just make her so anxious and uncomfortable she can't pray. Take a few demons and make her life too miserable to live."

Xada nodded his acknowledgement of the order and left. Baal smiled for the first time in several human days.

*****

Xada and the demons arrived in Huntersville and started watching the rental house. Max, Louis, and Eleanor were sleeping soundly. He sent demons to put Max and Louis in a deep sleep of nightmares and enjoyed watching the men grow restless. He smiled arrogantly as he sent demons to torment Eleanor.

Eleanor woke from a sound sleep to instant alertness. Something was wrong. Something bad was coming. Fear and dread were like a heavy weight on her shoulders and chest. She got out of bed, knelt beside the mattress and began to pray.

She prayed out loud in a commanding voice, "Jesus Christ is Lord of all and victorious over death and sin. In the name of Jesus Christ, I rebuke you Satan, Baal. I rebuke your fallen angels and demons. In the name of Jesus Christ, I command you to leave this house. Jesus, I ask for your protection. I ask for a hedge of almighty power and angels to surround our house. Lord, I pray that you will show Max and Louis the way and the truth, and that they will give their hearts back to you."

While Eleanor was praying, Xada swore as he watched his demons grow weak and flee. Curious, he backed away but watched the praying woman. She always wore the Christian aura that could only be seen in the spritual world, but tonight it was different, stronger. He angrily realized that she had someone else joining her in prayer. He needed to find out who that was.

Still feeling the need to pray, Eleanor repeated the same words over and over until she felt she could stop. When Eleanor crawled back into bed, she felt exhausted but at peace, and she fell asleep.

*****

Several miles away, Angela woke from a sound sleep to an instant alertness. She strangely felt the need to pray. But why? Angela jumped from the bed and got on her knees.

"Lord Jesus in Heaven, I don't know why you need my prayers, only you know that. Please join my prayers with those of the ones in trouble. Keep them safe from illness and harm. Give them peace and strength."

Angela repeated the words over and over until the pressing need to pray passed. When she crawled back into bed, she was exhausted and fell into a deep, peaceful sleep.

*****

The next morning at breakfast, Louis asked Max, "How did you sleep?"

"Terribly. I tossed and turned with nightmares all night," Max said.

Louis looked Max in the eye and said, "So did I." He paused, "I think we were visited last night. I woke up to a very familiar foul smell."

Max nodded, remembering the smell of Baal's

breath. Fear showed in the eyes of both men.

Eleanor walked in and sat at the table with a bowl of cereal.

"Did your Baal come to you in the night?" she asked the two men.

Looking concerned, Louis said, "We're not sure. We both had nightmares. Why?"

Eleanor nodded. "I think he tried. Something woke me up to pray. They tried to get to one of us. If not you two, then me. I'm sure he's angry that I stopped him when we were on the plane."

She looked at her brothers, "I'm tired. I don't know how much longer I can protect you two from him. You can get out of that contract, you know."

"How?" Max asked.

"Repent and accept Christ," Eleanor answered. "It's an unwritten loophole of love not mentioned in your contract. Ask for God's forgiveness. He is stronger than Baal and all his minions combined. Accept Christ as your Lord and Savior, and you'll overcome all of this," Assuming she had endured another skirmish in a spiritual war, Eleanor softly said, "Prayer 2, Baal 0."

CHAPTER 9

R ay and Brenda Sutton were already eating breakfast when Angela entered the kitchen. She walked in yawning.

"I need coffee," she said.

"Did you not sleep well?" Brenda asked.

Angela looked at her parents, "It was the strangest thing. I woke up in the middle of the night, instantly alert with the need to pray. I have no idea why or for whom, but I did. It felt like whatever was happening was urgent."

"I'm glad you listened to the spirit," Brenda said. "It's awesome when that happens."

"Well, last night was a little frightening. I don't know what was going on, but I think it had the potential to be very bad," Angela said as she picked up a sausage biscuit. "When do we get started? If we get through in time, I may have a date."

Brenda grinned, "Anyone we know?"

"No," Angela said. "We met on the plane coming back from California. It was instant friendship. His name is Michael, and he moved to Charlotte recently for his job."

"Who does he work for?" Ray asked.

"M & L Toys," Angela said. "I didn't know that at the time. He told me Monday night when he came to Durham to have dinner."

"He went all the way to Durham to take you to dinner?" Brenda asked with raised eyebrows.

"Yes. He apologized for not telling me on the plane, but he wanted to get to know me without the cloud of the toy company hanging over our heads. But it gets worse," Angela said.

"How?" Ray asked.

"He owns the company. It's Michael Jamison, who will be my boss in a little over a week," Angela told them.

"Oh," Ray said. "That could be a problem."

"Yeah, ya think?" Angela said rolling her eyes in exasperation. "I took the job anyway. If I find I need to leave the company because of awkwardness, at least I can put it on a resume. That's a plus."

"Do you like this man?" Brenda asked.

Angela nodded, "Very much. I would take a relationship with him over the job. He's that great."

"Is he a Christian?" Brenda asked.

Taking a deep breath, Angela said, "We haven't discussed that. It will be my number one conversation item tonight if we finish the combining in time."

Ray stood, "Well, let's get started. We'll plan to stop by lunch. It's Saturday, and we have other things to do, too. Mom and I can finish next week. There's not much left."

Before going out to the equipment garage, Angela texted Michael.

Angela: Good morning. Will finish at lunch. Afternoon free. Let me know what you'd like to do later.

The sound of a text notification woke Michael. He looked out the window. It was barely daylight. He looked at his phone. Angela? Wow, they really did start at daybreak.

He sat up and texted.

Michael: Working? Already? This early? Really? Wink emoji. Furniture arrives today. Will make a plan as soon as I know when the stuff is getting here.

Angela: LOL. Sorry if I woke you. Getting ready to start. Can't text until lunch. Call if you need to talk.
Michael: Will do.

*****

Baal watched Xada walking toward him.

"Well?" he asked. "What did you do and how miserable is that praying woman?"

"We couldn't get to her," Xada said with disgust. "I thought we had a chance in the middle of the night, but something woke her, and she started that infernal praying. But I think she had help."

"What do you mean help?" Baal asked.

"Her protection was stronger than usual," Xada said.

"Who was helping her?" Baal snarled.

"I couldn't tell. I do know that it wasn't her brothers," Xada said.

Baal lost his temper, and the whites of his eyes turned black. He bellowed and shouted obscenities. Foul spittle shot out of his mouth, almost hitting Xada. Xada calmly stepped aside and waited for Baal's tantrum to end.

"Find out who's helping her!" Baal commanded loudly. "I don't think it's her son. We've distracted him to the point he won't even think about praying."

Xada nodded and left. He was glad to be out of the presence of an angry Baal.

Chapter 10

Angela came into the house at noon. She showered to wash off the morning's dirt and sweat then went to the kitchen to find something to eat. She had just finished making a sandwich when her phone rang. She looked at the caller ID and smiled.

"Hey," she answered. "Did you get your furniture?"

Angela heard Michael's frustrated voice say, "No. They won't be here until around three which means it may be four. I can't go anywhere until after they leave."

"Well, that's frustrating," Angela said. "Want me to come over and keep you company?"

Michael smiled, "I would love for you to come and keep me company. I'll text you the address."

"Great!" Angela answered. "By the way, what

color is your kitchen?"

"It's black and white with silver appliances," he replied. "Why?"

"Well, I thought I would bring rags, dish soap and disinfectant wipes. We'll clean your kitchen and get it ready for your kitchenware," she said. "I'll see if we have any shelf liner in the pantry."

"You don't have to do that," Michael said.

"Hey, the quicker we get that done, the quicker we get to relax or go have fun somewhere. Do you have food?" she asked.

"Not much. I've mostly been eating out," he said.

"I'll bring snacks and drinks," she said. "We can order pizza for dinner if we're still busy by then."

"Angela, I don't want you to have to do all that. You've already put in a six-hour workday," Michael said.

"We'll work together, and it'll be fun," she said. "Now, I'm going to hang up so I can eat lunch and get going. Text me your address. I should see you in about an hour."

"Yes, Ma'am. I could use a decisive manager like you. Want to go to work for a toy company?" he asked teasingly.

Angela laughed, "Let me think about it. See

you soon." She ended the call.

Michael grinned. Angela was coming over.

A little over an hour later, Angela turned into Michael's driveway. He came outside to meet her. When she got out of the car, she started handing him bags.

"What's this?" he asked.

"Cleaning supplies and snacks," Angela said as she reached back into her car.

"You were serious about working, weren't you," he said laughing.

"Oh, yeah. I never kid about housework," she said and gave him a wink.

Michael felt his heart flip. Slow down, he told himself. They had only known each other for a week, but Michael's heart wasn't listening to his brain.

"Show me your house," she said smiling. "I've been wanting to see it."

Michael took her into the kitchen where they put the bags on the counter. He threw his hands out and started pointing.

"This is the kitchen. Laundry room through that door, pantry through that door, and you came through the mudroom which has a small bathroom with a shower," he said.

"I like this," she said. "Wide open workspaces

that ease into the dining and living areas." They walked through the dining area into the spacious living room.

Angela turned to the fireplace. "I think I'm in love. This is beautiful."

The gray colored stone fireplace reached up to the ceiling. The mantle was half of a wide cedar log. The top was smooth and polished, but the bottom was rounded and still rough.

Michael took her up the stairs. A balcony with a loft area ran in front of two bedrooms which had their own baths.

"This is a really nice house," Angela said.

"I'm used to condominiums," he said. "This is as big as I want for now."

"I like the deck that runs in front of the house on the upper level. It shades your patio below," she observed. "Michael, you picked out a great house. We just need to get your furniture and turn it into your home. Let's get started," Angela said and went back down the stairs.

For the next hour, they used disinfectant wipes to wash the shelves in the kitchen, laundry room, and bathrooms. Angela opened a bag and took out scissors and several rolls of shelf liner.

They had just finished lining the last shelf

when the moving van turned into his driveway. Michael directed the movers where to put the furniture. The boxes labeled "kitchen" were left with Angela. She started opening them and found his dishes, cookware, and kitchen towels. She laid a towel on the cabinet and started washing his silverware, glasses, and plates.

Eventually all the boxes and furniture were in the house, and the movers left. Michael came into the kitchen, and Angela handed him a soda on ice in a clean glass.

"You got all this done?" he asked.

"It's just your dishes. They're clean. You choose the cabinet you want to put them in," she said.

Michael took her hand and led her to the couch.

"Sit," he said. "We need a break. As for the kitchen, you organize it the way you think is best. I'm terrible in the kitchen."

"But you have great taste in décor," Angela said. "I love your furniture."

"I want comfort when I sleep and relax. The color didn't matter as much as that did. But I am not a decorator," he said laughing. "Half the stuff I own rarely matches."

Michael and Angela sat and talked. They enjoyed getting to know each other better and discovered more things they had in common.

Finally, Angela stood and said, "Break's over. Back to work."

Michael groaned, "But I'd rather sit and talk with you." He grabbed her hand and pulled her back down on the couch.

Angela was caught off balance. She gave a quick squeal and landed in Michael's lap. She was laughing when Michael put his hand on her cheek, turned her face to him and kissed her. That kiss was everything he had hoped it would be.

The kiss surprised Angela. It was the best kiss she ever had. No man she had dated kissed like that, nor had she reacted to them with a longing for more.

When she didn't object, Michael kissed her again. He decided he could spend a lifetime wanting those kisses.

Michael whispered, "I've been wanting to do that since we got off the plane in Charlotte."

Angela smiled, "I would be lying if I said that I hadn't, because I've been thinking about it, too."

"I haven't wanted anything all week as much as I have wanted your company," he said. "Being with you is fun, interesting, intriguing, easy, calming, and I could go on, but I don't think there are enough adjectives."

"I feel that way about you. We just clicked from the first time we spoke on that plane," Angela said. "But what do we do with this? I don't want to make things uncomfortable for you at the office, but I do want that job."

"Honestly, I doubt we'll see much of each other there. I usually only meet with department heads." Grinning he said, "I don't interact with you peons."

Angela laughed, "Peon? I guess you're right. I think I'm at entry level, so that would describe me perfectly."

"Let's just see how it goes," he said, "because I want to see you and pursue this relationship."

Angela sat up, looked at Michael and said, "So do I. But I have one question that could be a deal breaker."

"What?" he asked, furrowing his brow with concern.

"Are you a Christian?" Angela asked him.

Michael looked at Angela's expression. It was a mix of question, concern, and hopefulness.

He smiled, "Yes. I take it you are too?"

Angela nodded, "Yes." She gave a sigh of relief. "Belief in God is the basic tenant and foundation for my life. I'm glad you agree."

"I do," Michael said, nodding. "I'm not sure I could get through these stressful days without knowing God." He laughed, "My mother has been lecturing me for years about finding the right woman and not getting unequally yoked. I'm getting tired of the yoke conversation."

"I heard the same from my parents," Angela said with a chuckle. "Mom was always reminding me to find a boyfriend of similar faith."

Michael and Angela sat a few minutes in companionable quiet. Suddenly, Angela stood and pulled Michael to his feet,

"Come on," she said. "let's get to work and finish this."

Michael stood, kissed Angela and said, "Oh alright. If we must."

The two spent the next hour unpacking, organizing, washing dishes and cookware, filling closets, and putting out bath linens.

"Enough!" Michael exclaimed. "I need food. Let's go get a pizza."

"Can we do takeout?" Angela asked. "I'm not dressed to go out to eat. I'm in work clothes."

"Sure. I'll call it in. Loaded alright with you?" he asked.

"Yes," she answered. "Glad I brought paper

towels. You don't have any napkins."

Michael called in the order then handed Angela a notepad and a pen.

"Will you make a list of what I need to buy," he asked. "Everything from napkins to laundry detergent."

Angela laughed.

"What?" he asked.

"You asked for it," she said. "You may regret the extensive list that I give you."

"Nah, I'll just pick and choose what I want and gradually get it all," he said grinning. "Back in a bit."

Angela watched Michael walk out the door. She looked around at what else she could do. Seeing all the empty boxes, she smiled, took a knife and broke them down. She would take them to Durham, reassemble them, and use them to move her things.

The last box was in her SUV when Michael came back with the pizza. He walked into the house and looked around.

"What did you do with the trash?" he asked.

Angela smiled, "I broke down the boxes and put them in my car. I'm going to take them to Durham to move my things home, unless you want them."

"No, no," he said. "You're welcome to them. Pizza's here!"

Michael put the large pizza on the kitchen island while Angela got plates and silverware. After refilling their glasses with soda, they sat on barstools and ate at the island.

The two talked while they ate. Angela asked a lot of questions about the toy company, and Michael answered them.

Finally, Angela looked at her watch, "It's getting late. I need to go."

"What time did you get up this morning?" Michael asked.

"Five," she said and yawned. "Yep, need to go. I'll talk with you tomorrow."

Michael pulled her into his arms and kissed her. "Let me know when you get home safe."

Angela smiled, and said, "OK. Text you in a bit."

Michael watched her leave. He already missed her.

CHAPTER 11

The following week was passing quickly. Angela's replacement at the snack food company was eager to learn and grateful for the calendars and lists that Angela was leaving him. One evening while Angela was at home filling a box with her belongings, Michael called.

She sat on the couch and answered the phone, "Hey."

"Hey," Michael answered. "Still packing?"

"Yeah. Mom and Dad are coming Friday afternoon," she said. "We'll finish packing then load everything early Saturday morning."

"Need some help?" he asked.

"Sure," Angela said.

"Can I sleep on your couch?" he asked.

"Of course," she said smiling.

"Then I'll be there Friday evening and will

bring in supper," Michael said.

"Sounds great," Angela said with a smile.

"What does your family like to eat?" he asked.

"We eat anything," she said.

"Chinese?" he asked.

"That's perfect. We love Chinese," Angela answered.

"Alright," he said. "I'll bring several different entrees with rice and fortune cookies."

"I'll have drinks," Angela said. "Yay. I'm excited. I can't wait to see you, and you'll get to meet the parents."

"Should I be nervous?" he asked.

"Definitely not," she reassured him. "Dad will love having an extra set of muscles to load furniture. They're great parents and wonderful people. I know you'll like them. I'm confident they'll like you."

"Okay," Michael said. "Plan's made. It's getting late. You need to stop packing and get some rest."

"You don't have to tell me twice. I'm tired and ready for bed. Have a good evening. Good night," Angela said.

"Good night," Michael said and ended the call. He couldn't stop smiling. He had known Angela two weeks, and he was meeting the parents. It felt like he had known her his whole life.

*****

In his headquarters, Baal sat on an ostentatious throne, drumming his long, sharp fingernails on the arm of the chair. Nothing was going to plan, and he was highly annoyed and short tempered.

Calling Xada over, he asked, "Still can't get to the woman?"

"No," Xada answered, obviously frustrated.

"Let's change tactics," Baal said. "If I can't have that toy company, let's sow strife and create problems. We can make Michael Jamison so frustrated he wants to sell the business. See what you can do about that." Xada nodded and left.

Baal watched Xada leave. He smiled. Just thinking about making Michael Jamison miserable had brightened his mood, and he couldn't wait to hear the results of Xada's efforts.

*****

Thursday morning, Michael was looking at sales reports when Helen, the new administrative assistant, called to let him know George Martinez wanted to see him. Michael told her to send him in. George entered the office and closed the door. Michael could tell something was troubling George.

"What's on your mind?" Michael asked.

George sat in the chair across from Michael and said, "We've had an employee file a complaint against another employee."

"We've never had that happen before," Michael said, frowning. "What's the situation?"

"A newer employee in product development has filed a complaint against the manager. He claims she's forcing him to accept beliefs that aren't his," George said.

"What beliefs?" Michael asked.

"The newer employee, Jeffrey, complains that the manager, Sheila, is forcing him to believe in Christianity," George said.

"That doesn't sound like Sheila," Michael said. "Did you talk to her about it?"

"I did," George answered. "She said she doesn't do that. Sheila assigned Jeffrey to the team that develops products for the small line of Christian books and toys that we have. When he objected, she changed him to another area. She didn't force him to work on that small niche of merchandise. I told her to write and submit a rebuttal."

"Good plan," Michael said. "If Jeffrey pushes for a disciplinary action against Sheila, stall and let me know. I'll step in and talk with Jeffrey. The last thing we need is that sort of publicity."

"I agree," George said. "The other employees in that department are angry with Jeffrey. One came to me and told me what he saw and heard, and it matches Sheila's side of the controversy."

Michael said, "Keep me posted. Since it's a personnel issue, it needs to stay confidential, but something tells me Jeffrey is more than willing to talk about it."

After George left, Michael thought about the problem. Over the years, the company had hired every religion, race, and ethnicity in Southern California, and there had never been a problem before. Why now?

*****

On the first floor, Xada watched one of the demons whisper in Jeffrey's ear, making him irritable and discontented. The demon whispered that Jeffrey was right to resist Sheila's attempts to expose him to Christianity. Jeffrey threw down the pencil he was using and stormed out of the office. He climbed the stairs to human resources and demanded to see George.

George let Jeffrey into his office and closed the door, "What's the problem, Jeffrey. You look upset."

"What have you done about Sheila? I can't even sit in the same room with her because I'm afraid that she's going to start praying or singing hymns," Jeffrey complained.

"Jeffrey, she's not going to do that," George calmly told him. "I would ask you to realize that the small group of books and toys in question fits a niche in the population. It's a product line just like dolls or board games. No one is going to force any religion on you because that's not something we want in the company. You have submitted your report. I talked with Sheila, and she is submitting one as well. When I have both, I will meet with Mr. Jamison."

"Thank you." Jeffrey stood and quietly left the office. The conversation had not gone as he had hoped. The goal was to get rid of Sheila, not wait on reports and decisions. Not getting any satisfaction from his conversation with George made Jeffery feel tense and irritable. It was going to be a long afternoon.

*****

Michael sat at his desk wondering if Jeffery's complaint was an attack on the Christian faith. He called his mother.

"Michael!" Eleanor said with pleasure. "You never call during the workday. This is a pleasure, but I have to ask, is something wrong?"

Michael told Eleanor what was happening in the product development department.

"Is this an attack on Christianity?" he asked. "How do I deal with this?"

"I believe you're right," Eleanor replied. "The only way to fight what is happening is with prayer, the kind I taught you when fighting what could be the work of demons."

"That's what I thought," Michael said.

Eleanor said, "You hang up and pray. I'll do the same."

When the call ended, both Eleanor and Michael prayed out loud for the demons to leave the building and for God's protection.

*****

Xada was enjoying watching the demon influence Jeffery. Suddenly, the demon let out a loud, high pitched screamed and ran away. Xada felt himself getting weak, and he fled. That praying woman was at it again. Baal was not going to be happy.

CHAPTER 12

Angela finished her final work week at the snack food company. Mr. Thomas told her goodbye and wished her well, and her replacement expressed his gratitude for the help getting started. When Angela carried the small box of personal items out of the building, she suddenly felt excited. She was free for the moment and scheduled to start an exciting new job on Monday.

Angela grinned as she drove to her condo. Her excitement in Michael's coming to Raleigh to help her move gave her a sense of renewed energy. She was ready to get the moving done and be back home, but she admitted that she was extremely happy to be closer to Michael.

Not long after Angela got home, Brenda called to let her know they were in the parking lot.

Angela met them at the security door.

"Come on in," she said as Ray and Brenda entered the condo.

Brenda hugged her then asked, "Are you sad to be leaving here?"

"Not really," Angela said. "It's not home. I'm going to clean the place and turn it over to a property management company I've signed with. I'll sell it when I need a down payment on another house. Until then, I'll collect the rent."

"It sounds like you've thought everything through," Ray said.

"I hope so," Angela replied. "But what I haven't told you is that Michael is coming to help. He'll be here in a little bit, and he's bringing Chinese takeout."

"Ooh yum," Brenda said.

"I won't lie," Ray said, "I'll be glad to have an extra pair of strong arms to load that sofa and your dressers."

"I can't wait to meet him," Brenda said, smiling.

"You're going to love him," Angela said, grinning.

An hour later, Ray was packing the items in the spare bedroom as Brenda worked in the kitchen. While Angela was packing her clothes and toiletries, her phone rang. The caller ID said Michael.

"Hey! Are you here?" she asked with a big smile.

"In the parking lot," he answered. "Want to help bring the food in?"

"Be right there," she answered.

Angela told her parents that Michael and the food had arrived and that she was going to help him carry it all in. Angela hurried to the parking lot where Michael was getting out of his car.

She hugged him and with a big smile said, "I'm so glad you're here."

Michael smiled, "Me too. I'm ready to get you packed and moved back home so you will be closer to me." He gave Angela a quick kiss then handed her two plastic bags. "If you will carry these, I can get the rest."

A few minutes later, Angela and Michael walked into the condo with bags of Chinese food.

Angela said, "Mom, Dad, this is Michael. Michael these are my parents, Ray and Brenda Sutton."

Michael smiled, shook their hands and said, "It's nice to meet you. Angela said you guys like Chinese."

"It's great to meet you," Brenda said, "and yes, that food smells wonderful."

Angela announced, "Break time. Let's eat."

Brenda and Angela set out plates and poured drinks. The four sat around the dining table eating, talking, and getting to know each other. When they finished eating, the table was cleared, and the packing resumed.

Brenda left Michael to work in the kitchen, and she went into the bedroom to help Angela. Shortly after ten, everything was packed except for the linens they would use that night and supplies for eating breakfast. Angela filled four disposable cups with ice and soft drinks. They sat around the table, tired, but satisfied with their accomplishment.

"I can't thank y'all enough," Angela said. "It would've taken me a whole lot of weekends to slowly move everything."

Ray looked at Michael and smiled, "I'm glad you're here. Tomorrow will be a busy day. We have to load and then unload the furniture."

Angela looked at Michael, "I have a storage unit rented near our house. The furniture and boxes going there are labeled unit. The things I'm taking to Mom and Dad's house are labeled farm."

"It sounds like you have everything organized," Michael said.

"She does," Ray said as he yawned.

Ray declared he was tired and that it was time for bed. After making sure he had everything he needed in the spare room, Angela took linens and made the couch into a bed for Michael.

"You have a nice long couch," he said. "I fit on here just fine."

"Good," she said. "I'll see you in the morning."

Michael pulled her close and kissed her.

He whispered, "I like your parents. See you in the morning."

"Told ya," she said grinning. "Night."

*****

Angela woke up at her usual time, just as the sun was rising. She yawned and decided to go make coffee. Brenda was already awake.

Tiptoeing out to the kitchen, Angela started the coffee maker that she had prepped the night before. Michael watched her. She looked cute tiptoeing around in her t-shirt and sleep shorts.

"You don't have to try to be quiet. I'm awake," Michael said out loud.

Angela jumped, "Oh my gosh, you scared me. I wasn't expecting that."

Michael grinned and sat up.

Angela wanted to stare. Michael was in pajama pants and no shirt. His chest was sculpted and muscular. She almost had to pinch herself to keep from gawking, but there was no stopping the blush on her face that proved she was affected by the way he looked.

Michael smiled, realizing that Angela liked what she saw. What a boost to his ego.

Angela gave a little cough and said, "Coffee should be ready soon. I'm going to get dressed."

Unable to control the grin on his face, Michael got up and went to the bathroom to change his clothes.

The group sat around the table with coffee and sausage biscuits. As they ate, they made a plan for loading everything. Ninety minutes later, Angela stood in her empty condo.

"Sad?" Brenda asked, putting her arm around Angela in a sideways hug.

"No," Angela answered. "I've already texted the property management firm that the condo is empty. They have a key and will use their people to deep clean the place before they show it." She turned and looked at the others. "Let's go. The sooner we get there, the sooner this is finished."

Three hours later, they all sighed with tired satisfaction. The large furniture and the boxes marked 'unit' were inside the environmentally controlled storage unit. The boxes going to the farm were easily packed in Angela and Michael's cars.

With the move completed, Angela looked at Michael and her parents and said, "Lunch is on me. Let's go to the café."

A few minutes later, the four walked into the cool, air conditioned building. The aromas of vegetables, french fries, and hamburgers lingered in the air. Ray, Brenda, and Angela waved and spoke to the ladies in the kitchen and to most of the people sitting in the dining room. Michael was intrigued.

When the four had been seated at a table, Angela said, "Order anything you want. This is my 'thank you' to you for helping me. You can even get dessert."

Angela looked at Michael, "Today's special is country fried steak and gravy. I highly recommend it. Also, Hazel, who owns the café, makes the best pies. You need to try a piece of one."

After they ordered their food, Michael continued to get to know the Sutton family. He watched people who were coming in or leaving greet the Sutton's. Michael realized that he was getting a glimpse into a part of southern life he had no idea existed.

Later at the Sutton home, Michael helped unload the boxes marked farm into a spare bedroom on the second floor.

When everything was inside, Angela said, "It's done! Thank y'all so much."

Brenda hugged Angela, "I am so glad you're back home." She looked at Michael, "I know you didn't hire her, but thank you for moving your company here. That job got her back home."

"It has worked out well for everyone, I believe," Michael said, smiling.

Angela looked at Michael and asked, "Would you like to see the farm?"

"I would love to," Michael answered. "I've been curious ever since you told me this is how you grew up. I've never been on a working farm before."

"Well, let's get you introduced." She looked at Ray, "OK if I take the ATV?"

"Sure," Ray answered.

Angela got the key from a hook at the back door and said to Michael, "Come on, Mr. City Man. Let's make a country dude out of you."

Angela took Michael to the barn and equipment buildings.

"You weren't kidding when you called the combine big," Michael exclaimed.

Angela laughed, "I know. It's huge, but it cuts a lot rows of corn at the same time." She pointed to two slightly smaller machines. "Those are for the wheat and soybeans."

"Hop in," Angela said, motioning to the all-terrain vehicle.

Michael and Angela settled into the ATV. Angela backed it out of the shed, and they rode around the farm. Angela showed Michael the bare fields where wheat had been cut, green corn beginning to tassel, the pond, and the pastures with Black Angus cows. She stopped at a woven fence, got out, looked around and whistled. Four horses came running up.

Michael smiled when they came over and nuzzled Angela's cheek.

She laughed and said, "Alright. One at a time." Each horse got half an apple as a treat.

Angela pointed out her horse, Blazer; the stallion, Socks; and the mares, Star and Lois.

Michael pulled her close and kissed her.

"You are blessed," he said. "I'm glad you have the opportunity to move back home. There's a peace here. I never would have known what this was like if you hadn't shown me. Thank you."

Angela smiled, "I'm glad you like the farm. I would rather be here and commute to Huntersville than live in a condo across the street from the office."

"I can see that." Michael kissed her again. "I've wanted to hold you and kiss you all day.

"I've been thinking about that myself," she said grinning. "Come on, get back in the ATV. I have one more place to show you."

Angela drove into the woods and stopped in a clearing. A grove of trees framed a sandy creek bank in shade. The water near the bank flowed slowly, but the water on the other side of the creek ran quickly over rocks.

"This was my favorite place in the summer when I was a kid," she told Michael. "Mom would bring a book and a chair. She would read while I played."

"This is amazing," Michael said. "I can see you liking it here as a kid. I like it here, and I'm grown." The two sat in the ATV and talked.

Angela looked at her watch, "Oops, we need to go. Mom and Dad are grilling burgers for supper. I fed you at lunch; they'll feed you at dinner. Now you can say you work for food!"

Michael laughed, "That would be true today."

After dinner, which was outside on the picnic table, Angela and Michael sat in the front porch swing talking. The sun was setting, the crickets and katydids were chirping, and occasionally they heard a cow lowing in the pasture.

"It's so peaceful here," Michael said.

"Anytime you need to de-stress, you're welcome to come to the front porch swing," Angela said.

"Only if you're here, too," he said.

Michael kissed her then said, "I need to be going. I'm flying to California tomorrow with Mom and the uncles. I have some company business to take care of, and they're going to start packing. They found a house, and the owner accepted their bid."

"I'm happy for them," Angela said. "I know you're glad that they're moving here."

"I am. I'll be the one who looks after them as they age, and I'm glad I won't have to travel across the country to do it." He stood and said, "Why is it so hard to leave you? I just want to wrap you up and take you with me."

Angela smiled, "I know. I feel it too. Get your California business done and get back here soon. How long will you be gone?"

"Not sure. It depends on how fast I get the

work done," he said. "As soon as I have things finalized, I'll come back. Peter, my friend from college, is the electronic toys manager and is meeting me at the California factory to make decisions about selling the property and equipment. Our factories are small and specialized, and electronics is the first to move. Then we'll work on the others."

Michael kissed Angela and held her tight. "I'll call and text. You do the same."

"Count on it," she said. "See you when you get back."

Michael smiled and walked to his car. When he left the driveway, Angela went back into the house. She was exhausted. Brenda was in the kitchen when Angela walked into the room.

"Hey, Mom. Any more apple pie?" Angela asked.

Brenda smiled and pushed the pie plate toward her, "One piece left."

Angela got a fork and ate it from the plate.

"Dad and I like Michael." Brenda chuckled, "Ray said the way Michael looks at you made him want to ask him what his intentions were."

Angela laughed, "What! That's so funny."

"Michael is falling in love with you," Brenda said. "It's written all over his face. You aren't far behind."

Angela sighed, "I know, and it worries me. I really want this job and to do well in it. But I don't want anything awkward to spill over into it, nor do I want to start any gossip. I'm not sure how to handle everything. He's flying to California tomorrow. He may be gone two days or two weeks. It all depends on how long it takes to make decisions and finish the business of moving the company. I'm relieved that he won't be there Monday, so I won't be distracted."

"Be patient and take it slow. It'll all work out," Brenda said.

Chapter 13

Monday morning, Angela dressed professionally and entered the M & L Toy Company at 8:15 for her 8:30 orientation. Millie, the receptionist, directed her to the conference room on the third floor. Three people had already arrived when she got there and took a seat.

A man about ten years older than Angela, with glasses and premature gray at his temples, entered the room and sat down beside her.

He extended his hand and said, "I'm Blake Johnson."

Angela smiled, shook his hand and said, "Angela Sutton."

"I'm going to work in the marketing department, and you?" Blake asked.

Angela smiled, "I'm in the marketing department, too. It's nice to meet you."

"Do you know what you'll be doing?" he asked.

"No," she answered. "I just assumed it would be entry level. I only have two years' experience."

"I don't know either. I guess we'll see what strengths we all have and see how that shakes out," he said.

George Martinez came into the room carrying an armload of packets.

"It looks like we're all here now," he said. "Let's get started."

Everyone filled out the employee paperwork for the government and Human Resources. George gave an overview of the company and its products, then went over the pertinent and most important parts of the employee handbook. After a tour of the building, he dismissed everyone for lunch.

"Would you like to have lunch?" Blake asked Angela. "I know a good sandwich shop on Main Street."

"That would be great," she said. Angela got into the car with Blake, and he drove to the restaurant. They ordered and began the process of getting to know each other.

After lunch, the department managers came

in to give an overview of how their areas worked and contributed to the smooth running of the company. When it was Evie's turn to talk about marketing, Angela was disappointed. The woman read her presentation and never looked up. The orientation ended at four o'clock.

"We're finished with this part of the orientation," George told the group. "Your managers are expecting you and will show you where you'll be working."

Angela and Blake walked down the hall to the marketing department. Blake opened the door, and they walked in. Evie came out of her office, welcomed them, showed them where they would be working and gave them a key to the office.

Evie looked at the clock. "Go ahead and go home. It's too late to start anything today. Come ready to work tomorrow morning."

Blake and Angela said goodbye and rode the elevator to the lobby.

As they started to go out the door, Blake asked, "What do you think of Evie?"

"I don't know her well enough to make a decision about her on anything," Angela replied. "Why?"

"Oh, I just wasn't impressed," he said. "She's

going to have to work hard to overcome a poor first impression with me."

Angela nodded and said, "I see what you're saying, and I agree. She could have presented her information a little better. Hopefully, she runs her department smoothly." Angela reached her car, turned to Blake and said, "I'll see you tomorrow morning." Blake waved and got into his car.

*****

Upstairs in the building, Xada watched as the demon he appointed to cause mischief whispered into Evie's ear.

"Watch out for that Angela," the demon whispered with a hiss. "She'll get your job if you're not careful. She's a spoiled, southern belle who thinks she's perfect and will pout if she doesn't get her way. So immature. You need to make her miserable enough to quit the job."

Evie Barone looked at the office with its empty desks. She was irritated that Angela had even been hired and decided to give the unwanted woman all the boring, entry level tasks. She smirked at her plan. Hopefully, that would frustrate Angela enough to leave the company.

*****

The next morning, Angela woke with a smile.

She had talked with Michael for a long time the night before and had let him know just how much she missed him. Her feelings for him just kept growing.

Eager to start the day, Angela got dressed and drove to the office. She pulled into the lot and parked beside Blake who had just arrived. They greeted each other and entered the marketing office just before eight. Angela put her purse away, then she and Blake knocked on Evie's door.

"Come in," Evie said.

Blake and Angela sat in the chairs in front of Evie's desk.

"I have given you each an assignment," Evie said. "I want it finished or as near to finished as possible by five. Angela, here is a list of toys and a list of competing companies. I want you to research their prices by region. Blake, here is a list of the newspapers and magazines where we buy ad space. I want an advertisement for each one."

"What are we advertising?" Blake asked.

"Toys," Evie said.

"Anything special?" Blake asked. "A specific toy going on sale, a new toy coming to the market?"

"No," Evie said. "Just toys."

"How big of an ad?" he asked.

"Big enough to catch the eye," she said.

"Is there a budget for these ads that I need to stay within?" he asked.

"Just develop the ads. I'll worry about the budget," she said.

Blake and Angela looked at each other and left Evie's office. Their desks were beside each other.

"I'm confused," Angela said. "I have a low-level task that I never did in my last job because the delivery people brought that information back from the stores. I would bet our store managers keep up with this information, too. You have a huge task with no guidelines that you can't finish in two days. Am I missing something?"

"If you are, then I am, too," Blake said.

"Well, it'll take me all of one hour to do this, then I'll help you. Get organized, and I'll hurry and finish this task," Angela said.

Within an hour, Angela was finished. "OK, Blake. What are we doing?"

"I called the logistics department," Blake said. "They sent me a list of toys that the stores are running sales on this weekend as well as the location of the stores. I thought we could start with newspaper ads for those sales."

Angela looked at the list of toys and the store locations. She took some paper from the copier and began sketching a basic template then changed the look for the different regions of the country.

"I like that," Blake said. "Let's add some other toys in the background. Do you use a publishing program?"

"Yes," she said nodding. "I'm not good at graphic design."

Blake opened the program and began to copy the toys from a company catalogue and placed them on the ad. They began to individualize the ads to different regions of the country.

Blake and Angela were so focused on what they were doing that they didn't hear Evie come up behind them.

"What are you doing?" Evie asked abruptly.

Blake looked up, surprised at Evie's tone.

He replied, "We're developing the ads you wanted."

Evie looked angrily at Angela and with venom in her voice said, "I didn't tell you to do that! Why aren't you working on the task I gave you? You should be doing what I assigned, not helping another employee because you don't like your assignment."

Angela looked shocked, "But Evie, I...."

Evie interrupted Angela and said, "You're fired. If you can't take direction, you can't work here."

Angela looked at Blake in shock. Blake looked just as baffled.

"Well," Evie said, "what are you waiting for? I don't need someone who can't follow directions."

Angela slowly stood, got her purse and left the department. She couldn't believe what had just happened. It took everything she had to not react as she walked to the elevator. Angela felt attacked, and the more she thought about the look on Evie's face, the sicker her stomach felt.

Evie went back to her office feeling triumphant. The southern belle with her annoying accent was gone.

Blake watched Evie sit behind her desk and was annoyed with the woman's obvious pleasure at what she had done. He sat in disbelief at what had just happened and was suddenly unsure he could work with someone so irrational. Reaching over to Angela's computer, Blake printed two copies of Angela's finished task, folded them, and put them in his pocket. Then he shut the computer down, hoping it would prevent Evie from deleting Angela's work.

*****

Xada smiled, stroked Evie's head and whispered to her that she was right to fire Angela. He whispered that Angela would be a temperamental employee who would try to get Evie's position. He congratulated her on a job well done. Evie smiled.

Xada was pleased. He knew Angela was a Christian. She had the aura that Christians wore. His demons had caused company strife and strife for a Christian. This had been a good day's work, and it wasn't even lunchtime yet.

*****

Angela was still in shock. She took the elevator to the second floor and went to Human Resources. She was shaking as she asked to see George Martinez.

George came out of his office, smiled, then immediately frowned when he saw the look on Angela's face.

"Angela, what's wrong?" he asked with concern.

It was taking every ounce of strength Angela had to not burst into tears. Her hand trembled as she handed him her badge.

"Why are you handing me this?" he asked.

"Evie fired me," Angela said, her voice trembling.

George looked shocked, "Why?"

"I was helping a coworker," Angela said. Then she turned and left the office before the tears that were welling in her eyes fell down her cheeks.

George frowned with confusion and disappointment. He put the badge on his desk then went to the third floor. He needed to get the whole story. George went to Evie's office and closed the door.

"Why did you fire Angela Sutton?" he asked. "She's only been here two days."

Evie looked at George with a smug expression, "I knew she wouldn't work out. She didn't do what I assigned her. Instead, she chose to work on a different assignment that wasn't hers. I don't need anyone who won't follow directions."

George nodded and left her office. His gut told him there was something very wrong and that he had not gotten the whole story from Evie.

He walked to Blake's desk and asked, "Can you

tell me what happened?"

Blake said, "Evie gave Angela a clerical assignment. She gave me an assignment that couldn't be finished in two days. She wanted both by five. Angela finished her task in one hour." Blake took the paper from his pocket, "Here's a copy of it. When she finished, she started helping me. With Angela's help, we have a fantastic sales ad specific to the different regions of the country. It'll be finished by five."

Blake paused, then said, "George, I don't think Evie wanted Angela working here in the first place. She didn't even give Angela a chance to tell her that she had finished what Evie had given her to do. Actually, she was completely irrational, and I'm wondering if I should start looking for another job."

George said, "Thank you, Blake. You're an asset to this company, so please don't resign. I promise I'll figure this out." George shook Blake's hand and left the department.

CHAPTER 14

Brenda looked up in shock when Angela walked into the kitchen in the middle of the day.

"Why are you home?" she asked.

"I got fired," Angela said miserably, tears filling her eyes.

"Fired! Why?" Brenda asked incredulously and looking shocked.

"I don't know," Angela answered, her voice trembling. "I did everything Evie wanted me to do and started helping my coworker who was overwhelmed. She got angry that I was helping Blake and fired me, right there on the spot. I didn't even get a chance to tell her that I had finished the task she wanted me to do."

Brenda walked over and pulled her daughter

into a hug. "That doesn't sound right. What are you going to do?"

"I'm going to change, go for a ride on Blazer, and somewhere along there I'm sure I will cry. I should have stayed at the snack food company. At least everyone liked me there," she said and slowly climbed the stairs to her bedroom.

Angela changed, left her cellphone in her room and walked to the barn. She didn't feel like talking to anyone. Inside the barn, Angela leaned up against one of the stalls and sobbed. She was hurt, and she was embarrassed.

"Oh, God, help me," she cried aloud. "I don't know what I did, but I need you. I need your peace and your strength, and I need your guidance to know what to do next."

Angela opened the gate to the pasture, stepped inside and whistled. Blazer came galloping across the pasture. When Blazer was saddled, Angel mounted the horse and started riding through the farm roads and trails.

*****

George Martinez called Angela's cellphone number. He was determine to correct the situation. She didn't answer, so he left a message. He tried again thirty minutes later. Still no answer. George looked through her file and found an alternative number. He called that.

The Sutton house phone rang, and Brenda answered it. "Hello?"

"May I speak with Angela Sutton please? This is George Martinez calling from M & L Toys."

"I'm sorry, but she isn't here," Brenda said. "She came home upset, changed her clothes and went for a ride on her horse. She hasn't come back, and I honestly don't know when to expect her."

"Will you have her call me as soon as she comes back in?" he asked.

"I'll give her your message, but I can't force her to call," Brenda said. "I understand she no longer works for your company, and she's quite upset about that."

"I understand, and thank you for giving her the message. I want to hear her side of the story and do my best to fix things," George said and ended the call.

He was frustrated. Evie was happy with what she had done. A good employee had left a secure position for M & L Toys and was now going to have to look for another job. He would keep trying to contact Angela.

*****

Xada approached Baal.

"What's happening at the toy company?" Baal asked.

Xada smiled, "One employee has filed a grievance against another, but the best part of this day was when we got a Christian fired."

Baal rubbed his hands and smiled, "That's tantalizing. I wish I could have seen that. Was the Christian upset?"

"I think so," Xada said. "She tried hard to hold it together, but I'm sure she has cried a few tears."

"Aww, Boo Hoo," Baal said sarcastically. "Poor little Christian got her feelings hurt." He smiled, "Now that's what I like to see!"

*****

Ray was in the barn when Angela returned from her ride.

"Angela?" he asked with concern. "Are you alright? Mom said you had a pretty bad day at work."

"Bad doesn't begin to describe it, Dad," Angela said as she unsaddled Blazer. "The biggest mistake I have ever made was applying for a job at

M & L Toys."

"What about Michael?" Ray asked.

"I can't talk to Michael right now," she answered. "What happened today is not his fault, and I need to be able to talk about it without either crying or getting mad."

Ray nodded, "That's wise. Take your time and find the right job. In the meantime, I can use the help around here. I'll even pay you."

Angela smiled, "I'll help you, Dad. No worries."

"We could expand things on the farm; go into business together," Ray said. "We could both make a good living here."

Angela nodded. "Thanks, Dad. I may take you up on it. I'm pretty soured on marketing at the moment. That manager had a personal problem with me, and I hate that I will never know what it was." Angela walked back into the house.

"Feel better?" Brenda asked.

"A little." Angela smiled. "Dad wants me to go into business with him and expand the farm operations. I might do that. I'm not going to rush into another marketing job until I feel better about things. I'll be a farmer instead."

"George Martinez called," Brenda said, "and he wants you to call him back. I told him that I would give you the message, and I have. Now you do what you want to do."

*****

Michael was tired. It had been an extremely busy day, but he was making progress. All he wanted to do was get back to Charlotte and see Angela. He smiled, took out his phone and texted.

Michael: How did your day go?

He changed clothes and went downstairs to the kitchen. Angela had not texted back. She usually either texted quickly or called. He hoped nothing was wrong.

"You look troubled," Eleanor said to Michael.

"I texted Angela, but she hasn't texted back or called. She usually does either one within a few minutes," Michael told her. "I'm starting to worry."

Eleanor smiled, "Don't worry. I'm sure everything is fine. She may just be doing something where she can't talk. Maybe her phone died. Don't borrow trouble, Son."

Michael nodded, "You're right. She'll text back eventually."

CHAPTER 15

Wednesday morning, Angela began working on the farm full time. She knew that sulking and dwelling on being fired would do her no good. Plus, Ray needed the help, and she needed a job. She still felt an overwhelming hurt and anger over what happened at M & L Toys, but the thoughts of partnering with her father motivated her.

Angela's task for the day was to spray the the empty wheat fields to get them ready to plant soybeans. The day was hot, and Angela was grateful for the air conditioned tractor cab. She felt herself relax and was also grateful for the peace she was finding as she worked on the farm.

*****

That evening, Angela showered and got ready for bed. Finally, after two days, she looked at her phone. There were several missed calls from George Martinez. He kept asking her to call him back, but was there any point? She had been fired. There was nothing to discuss.

Michael had texted several times and tried to call her. She knew she didn't want to lose him, but she wasn't ready to talk with him. Angela decided to text Michael.

Angela: Sorry. Things are crazy here. No worries, just can't talk.

Angela turned her phone off and went to bed. She was exhuasted from the week's drama and farm work. An uninterrupted night's sleep was what she needed.

Michael heard his phone announce a text. Finally, Angela had replied. He felt relieved until he looked at the text. What was that about? Was she pushing him away? Even when she was in the wheat field she could talk. He felt his heart sink with worry and replied.

Michael: Too late. Worried. Will you call?

Thirty minutes later, Angela still hadn't called. His text hadn't even been read. She must have gone to bed. Michael was frustrated. This was totally unlike Angela. Something had to be very wrong. As hard as he tried to focus on something else, the worry that Angela was going through something difficult was eating at him.

*****

The next morning Michael called the office and asked for George.

When he answered, Michael said, "George, it's Michael. How are things going there?"

George sighed, "We're fine, except the product development department is still tense with a standoff between the manager and the employee. Angela Sutton and Blake Johnson started working on Monday. On Tuesday, Evie gave some very unequal assignments. Angela finished hers and started to help Blake. She's a team player.

"Evie got angry and accused Angela of not doing what she was ordered to do. Evie fired her. Second day on the job and the girl was fired for no good reason. When I investigated it, Blake handed me a copy of the assignment that Angela had finished for Evie." George sighed. "Evie has never wanted her from the beginning, but I don't know why. I think Evie is intimidated by her. I've tried for two days to get in touch with Angela to hear her side of the story, but she's not returning phone calls."

Michael was frustrated that he was not in Charlotte.

He said, "George, I can't get back there for several more days. Keep trying to reach Angela. You know she has to be upset. I don't blame her for not wanting to talk with anyone from M & L Toys. Does Evie have anyone else starting Monday?"

"Yes. Two more are starting on Monday," George said. "Evie chose these two, so there should be no problems. Blake Johnson said he and Angela would have made a good team. They were going to finish in one day what would have taken him two or more to do alone. They designed a fresh new ad to promote the sales this weekend, and Blake gave Angela the credit for it. I really want to repair the damage Evie caused."

Michael said, "Keep Blake Johnson happy if you can. We can't lose him, too. Thank you for working so hard to resolve this issue. Can you transfer me to Evie?"

"Sure," George said.

Michael waited then heard, "This is Evie Barone."

"Evie, this is Michael Jamison. I called to find out the status on the ads for the sales starting this weekend. I haven't seen any in the newspapers out here."

"Michael, they're in the process of being developed," Evie lied. She held the thumb drive that Blake had given her Tuesday afternoon with the ads ready to email. She would have to send them out today.

Stunned, Michael felt like Evie had just lied to him. Her story didn't match what George told him.

He said, "They should be in the paper today and tomorrow. Why are they not there, Evie? We can't sell toys if no one knows they're on sale."

"I promise, they'll go to the papers tomorrow," Evie said.

"Evie, tomorrow is Friday. The ad won't be out until Saturday. It will be too late. When I get back, I want a full report as to why you didn't get those ads done," Michael said angrily and ended the call.

Evie was worried. She needed to cover herself. Her whole purpose for the vague instructions and the delay sending the ads was to make Angela and Blake look like poor, inefficient workers. She would find a way to make sure Michael blamed them for the lack of advertisement and not her.

*****

Xada watched one of the demons soothe Evie and whisper in her ear that Angela was at fault, not her. He smirked as Evie's composure calmed and she practiced the lies she would tell to blame everything on Blake and Angela. Xada smiled; this was going well.

*****

After talking with George, Michael was even more concerned about Angela. He was outraged at what Evie had done, and he understood why Angela would not talk with him. Michael felt his stomach clench when he thought about what Angela was going through. He desperately wanted to talk with her, because he didn't want to lose her. He texted her again hoping she would reply.

Michael: Called the office. Heard what happened. Are you ok?

Angela looked at the text. She sighed. She

couldn't avoid him any longer.

She texted: No, but I will be.

Michael: Can we talk?

Angela: No. Can't talk about it.

Michael: Can we talk at all?

Angela: Not yet. Still too hurt, embarrassed, and angry. Not going to drag you into it.

Michael: If I fix it, will you come back?

Angela: Right now, I would say no. Got a bad taste in my mouth for M & L Toys. Been treated unfairly. I don't want anything to do with the company and absolutely will not work for Evie Barone.

Michael: OK. Can we talk anyway?

Angela: Not yet. The conversation will just go to the job. Don't want that. I'll be fine. I just need time and space to calm down. Got to go help Dad.

Michael felt helpless. He was thousands of miles away and couldn't do anything about what happened until he got back in the office. He was frustrated that all this had happened while he was in California, and he was afraid Angela wouldn't talk with him because, basically, he was M & L Toys. It was his company. What happened could affect their relationship, and he didn't want that because he was in love with

Angela Sutton.

*****

Angela felt guilty about not wanting to talk with Michael, but she knew he would want to hear her side of what happened, and she just didn't feel like talking about it. Well, it didn't matter anymore because she no longer worked there. She just wanted to get past it all. Unfortunately, that wish did nothing to ease the hurt she still felt. Putting her phone on silent, Angela loaded seed and fertilizer into a planter then drove to the fields to plant soybeans.

The whole time Angela was in the field, she prayed. She prayed for peace, for guidance, and for forgiveness if she had been at fault. She prayed for help in forgiving Evie and for the ability to not blame Michael. It wasn't Michael's fault, but he owned the company. To see Michael right now would just reopen the wound.

*****

Xada checked in on the Christian and saw that she was working on a farm. He was angry. He had cost her the job, but she was praying. Her aura was strong, and the spirit was near. Xada fled.

Baal saw Xada return and motioned him over.

"Tell me what's happening with my toy company."

Xada reported, "There's turmoil in the company, and Michael is in California. He's not at the office to correct any problems. Also, we will cost him money this weekend. The marketing manager did not get the sale ads out in time." Xada smiled, "She will blame the other employees."

"What about the Christian that lost her job?" Baal asked.

"She's still upset which means she won't return calls or even see Michael, but I couldn't get close. She is a praying Christian. The spirit was strong around her," Xada said in a disgusted voice.

"Well, at least she's not at the company to pray there," Baal said, snarling. "That's in our favor."

CHAPTER 16

On Sunday, Angela sat listening to the pastor preach his sermon. She tried hard to concentrate on what he was saying, but she was failing. It had been six days, and she was still reliving the moment Evie told her she was fired.

Angela felt guilty because she knew her parents were worried about her. Also, she knew that eventually she would have to talk with Michael, and she was afraid about how she would react.

She prayed, "Oh, Lord, I just want to forgive and forget. Please help me."

*****

Michael, feeling exhausted, was finally on his way back to Charlotte. It had been a long week, but he had gotten a lot done. Also, worrying about Angela had given him several sleepless nights. He laid his head back against his seat and tried to sleep. That would at least make the flight go by faster.

Michael was relieved when he finally landed in Charlotte. It was almost six o'clock when he got into his SUV in the airport's long term parking lot. He took the phone from his pocket and texted Angela.

Michael: Just got back. Can I come see you? Want to make sure you're OK.

Angela read the text. She felt her stomach drop and her chest tighten. She started to cry.

"Why can't I get over this!" she whispered aloud with annoyed frustration.

As much as she liked Michael, she was afraid if she saw him, she would either cry or be so angry she would refuse to talk. She sighed. May as well get it over with. She texted Michael back.

Angela: OK

Michael let out a long breath in relief. He texted her back.

Michael: Will be there as soon as I can.

Angela went to her room to change. She could at least look good during her breakdown. An hour later, Angela saw Michael's SUV coming up the driveway. Her nerves flipped in her stomach as she walked out onto the porch to meet him.

Michael saw Angela come out the door toward his car. She looked so sad that his heart broke. Michael got out and walked toward her. He wanted nothing more than to take her in his arms, but he held back, unsure of how she would react.

"Thank you for letting me come talk with you," he said.

Angela nodded.

"Want to walk?" he asked. Angela nodded again, and they walked toward the barns.

Michael asked, "Will you tell me what happened at the office?"

Angela shook her head no. Michael saw the tears running down her cheeks. His heart ached. He hated to see her cry.

Angela was angry at herself. She wanted to be mad and powerful, not weak and crying. She also knew she wouldn't be crying if Michael hadn't come.

Wiping her eyes, Angela said, "Sorry. I thought I was all cried out."

Michael felt guilty. He could do nothing to help her feel better, and the company he owned was at the root of her sorrow. Michael pulled her into his arms and just held her.

"Will you please tell me?" he whispered.

Angela sighed, moved away from Michael and crossed her arms as if in emotional protection.

"Evie called Blake and me into her office," she said. "She gave me a clerical job to do. I didn't even do that task at the snack food company because the delivery guys brought the information back to senior management. She gave Blake a list of all the papers the company uses to advertize and wanted him to do a sales ad. She didn't even tell him which toys he was supposed to promote. It was a huge job that had no direction or objective, and she wanted it by five.

"I finished my task in one hour then began to help Blake. Evie came over, saw that I was helping Blake and blew a gasket. She yelled at me for not doing the work I was ordered to do, but she never gave me the chance to prove that I did. She just fired me. She didn't even give me a chance to defend myself, so I took my name badge to George and left. That's it. My whole career at M & L Toys in a paragraph."

"Thank you," Michael said. "Thank you for sharing, and I'm so sorry you went through that. George has heard Evie's point of view. Blake managed to copy the report you did so she couldn't delete it and make it look like she was right. Blake is angry about this, too. He liked working with you. But no one has heard your side of all of this, and that to me is unfair."

Angela walked to the pasture fence where Blazer was waiting to be given a snack.

"Sorry, boy, I don't have any," she whispered sadly as she ran her hands along his head and ears.

Michael walked over and leaned on the fence. "What do you want to do? Do you want to file a complaint and get your job back? Do you want to forget M & L Toys and move to another job?"

"I don't know, Michael," Angela said, slightly irritated. "I can't file a complaint and get my job back. I can never go back there. You and I have been seeing each other in a relationship outside the office. If anyone found out about that, I would get the reputation of whining to the boss to get my way, or worse, sleeping with the boss to get my job. My ability to work at M

& L Toys is completely over. I may be angry at the situation, but I won't do anything that could reflect badly on you. Don't expect me to."

Michael felt helpless because everything Angela said was true. She described the situation exactly as it was and what it would be. The person he cared most about in the world had been deeply hurt and humiliated by an employee at the company he owned. It devastated him.

"Angela I care about you," Michael said. "I want to help make this better."

Angela took a deep breath, trying not to lose her temper.

She looked at him and said, "Michael, I care about you, too, I really do, but right now I don't want to talk about M & L Toys or to anyone at M & L Toys. My career died at your company. I now have a termination on my employment record, and that is a death sentence for a career. My vision for myself and my future ended, and I'm grieving. I will get over it, and I will pick up the pieces, but right now, don't ask me what that will be because I don't know."

Michael felt his heart sink into his feet.

"Does anyone at M & L include me?" he asked quietly.

Tears started to fall from Angela's eyes.

"Michael," she said, her voice trembling slightly. "I'm not blaming you for this. You had nothing to do with it. But you are M & L Toys. It's your company. Unfortunately, when I see you, I see M & L. I see you, and I see Evie yelling at me and firing me. I see you, and I feel all of that over and over. That's so unfair to you. I'll get through this, and I will rise above it, but you are going to have to be patient. If I had made a mistake, I would hold myself accountable and understand a termination. But this was a personal attack. That's what's so bad. I did nothing wrong except be someone that Evie Barone didn't like."

Michael had never panicked in his life, but right now he was beginning to know what that felt like. He felt on the edge of losing Angela, and he couldn't let that happen. He took her in his arms.

"I understand," he said. "I don't like it, but I understand. I won't force you to move through this faster than you need to. I'm angry at what happened for a multitude of reasons, but the fact that you were hurt by my company infuriates me. Knowing that what happened at my company could change our relationship terrifies me. I care for you, Angela, and I don't want to lose you or the wonderful relationship we've been building. That is more important to me than anything, even M & L Toys."

Relief spread through Michael when he felt Angela relax in his embrace and put her arms around his waist. Maybe they could get through this.

*****

Xada watched Michael and Angela. He hadn't realized there was affection there. That concerned him, and he decided he needed to end their relationship or Baal would never get his company back.

Chapter 17

Monday morning, Michael arrived at his office early but didn't park in his reserved space. He entered a side door and took the stairs to the third floor. Anger fueled his energy.

Helen, his assistant, walked into the office. She saw the light on under Michael's door and opened it.

"Michael!" she exclaimed. "I didn't know you were back."

Michael motioned for her to come in and close the door.

"I'm back," he said, "but I don't want anyone in the building to know I'm here. I have a few surprises to take care of, so please take messages and act as if I'm still in California. I'm going to call George Martinez. When he comes, just send him on in."

Helen smiled, "It's good that you're back. I'll keep your secret until you tell me otherwise."

"Thank you," Michael said. He waited a few more minutes then called George.

"This is George Martinez."

"George, it's Michael. No one knows I'm back but you and Helen, and I want it to stay that way. Can you come up here?"

"On my way," George replied.

George went to the third floor, entered Michael's office and closed the door. George sat in a chair in front of Michael's desk and handed Michael a folder.

"I was pretty sure you wanted to see this," George said.

The file held everything George had collected on the problems in the product development department and the marketing department. He sat back and waited while Michael read every word on every page.

When he had finished reading, Michael closed the folder, sat back and looked at George.

"Is this Jeffrey in product development a new employee or did he move from California?" Michael asked.

"We hired him here. His credentials are outstanding, but that's of no use if he can't get along with staff," George said.

Michael said, "I agree. I also believe putting Evie in management was a mistake. Do you think this Blake Johnson would make a good manager?"

"Absolutely," George said. "He's been Angela Sutton's biggest champion. He's furious over Evie's behavior. Just having talked with him during all this tells me he's management material. He knows his craft, and he knows how to treat people."

"Let's handle marketing first," Michael decided. "I'll go into your office from the back stairs. Then I want you to call Evie to come in. She failed to get advertisements for the weekend sales to the papers, and I'm pretty sure she lied to me about it in our phone conversation. We ought to fire her, but let's offer her the opportunity to stay employed, just not as manager. Or she can resign. I'm still trying to decide about Jeffrey in product development."

George stood, "I'll go downstairs and wait for you. When you get there, I'll call Evie." He left the office.

Michael took out his cellphone and called Eleanor.

"Michael?" she answered sleepily. "Is everything alright?"

Michael said, "I'm so sorry to wake you, Mom, but I need your help."

"What's going on?" Eleanor asked, instantly awake.

"Mom, I really think there is a spiritual battle taking place in this company," Michael said. "Anything Christian is being targeted. I need to handle some of these issues with the personnel director. Will you pray for me and this company?"

"Yes. I agree with you, Michael. I can almost guarantee that you are being attacked by the devil himself," Eleanor said. "I will pray. Call me when it's all over."

"Thanks, Mom. I'll let you know," Michael said and ended the call.

Michael placed his head in his hands and prayed out loud, "Lord, God, there is a battle here. Your people are being persecuted, and I don't know why. Please put your hedge of protection around our company and the employees." Then he said, "Jesus is Lord of all. He overcame sin and death. In Jesus' name I command every demon in this place to leave. Leave this building and my people. I rebuke you Satan and ask God to bind you away from this company. Thank you, Lord, for your blessings and your protection. Amen."

Feeling prepared, Michael took the stairs to George' office.

*****

Xada watched as the demons he had placed all over the building to cause strife started screaming and fleeing. Then he began to feel weak. That praying woman was at it again. He was so angry he knocked over the potted plants in the lobby as he fled.

Millie looked up in shock as a shadow passed over the lobby. The door to the outside flew open, and the plants blew over. What was that? She shook her head and got up to clean the mess.

*****

Michael entered the human resources department, and George called Evie to his office.

Evie had been feeling good about her position and decisions. George was going to want to talk about hiring a few more staff members. She smiled, walked into the human resources office and knocked on his door.

George opened the door and said, "Come in Evie. Have a seat."

"Thank you," Evie said and sat in the chair George indicated.

She smiled, "What can I do for you?" She looked around, saw Michael, and her smile vanished. She looked at George and asked, "What's going on?"

Michael sat in the other chair in front of the desk and said, "Evie, I was informed that you had a problem with an employee last week and fired her. I would like for you to tell me about it."

Evie told him her version of the incident.

"Did you give Ms. Sutton a chance to defend herself and prove she had done her work?" Michael asked. "Most managers would."

Evie knew she hadn't given Angela that chance, but she didn't want Michael to know it, so she lied.

She said, "I thought I did. She didn't respond so I just assumed she hadn't finished it."

Michael handed her the report Angela had finished. Evie was shocked. She was sure she had deleted it when the office was empty.

"This looks like what I wanted," Evie said. "Why didn't she just give it to me?"

"Did you give her a chance?" Michael asked.

"Of course. She said nothing," Evie replied,

lying again. Evie hadn't given Angela a chance to speak at all.

"Did you scold an employee for being a team player and helping another employee?" Michael asked.

"I scolded her because I was under the assumption that she had neglected the task I gave her so she could help Blake who had a much more desirable marketing task," Evie said.

"Why was that?" Michael asked.

"Why was what?" Evie asked, feeling confused and irritated.

"Why did Blake have a much more desirable task than Ms. Sutton? They were equals and should have had equal tasks," Michael said.

"I didn't think Angela had the knowledge base to accomplish what I gave Blake to do," Evie said defensively.

Michael nodded, then said, "Now, I would like to know why you didn't get the sale ads in the papers on time last week. They should have been to the papers days before they got there so they could be printed and put into circulation." He paused. "Also, I got a call from regional managers complaining that the sale ads weren't in the papers for their stores, either."

"We were short staffed," Evie said, making excuses. "Then there was the problem with Angela Sutton. Blake just didn't get them done in time."

"But you are responsible for everything in the department. You could have gotten them in earlier by helping Blake," Michael said, looking directly into Evie's eyes.

"Michael," Evie said, "This is not my fault. Those two employees were not capable of getting the job done."

Michael could feel his skin flush with anger. He realized that Evie was never going to take responsibility for her department. Plus, he was convinced she had lied to him several times in their conversation.

Taking a deep breath, Michael calmly said, "Evie, you are the manager. Everything in that department lands on your desk. You are responsible for delegating tasks and making sure everything is done in a timely manner. We lost sales because the ads never got to the papers."

Evie began to worry. She had been sure that she had covered herself for holding the ads back. Now, she wasn't as confident as she was when she walked into the office.

Michael said, "Evie, I am removing you from the position of manager of marketing. I'm going to promote Blake Johnson in your place. You may stay with the company as an entry level employee."

Fury flushed through Evie's body. "But that's not fair!" she countered loudly.

"Oh, I think it's very fair," Michael replied. "I could fire you for several reasons, but I will give you a second chance. Your second chance is in the form of an entry level employee."

"What if I don't want that demotion?" she asked defensively.

Michael said, "Evie, your choices are to accept the position I offered or resign. Those are your only two choices."

"Those choices are not acceptable!" Evie exclaimed. "You can't do this. Why such a hullabaloo over a spoiled southern belle whose accent grates on the nerves?"

Michael was surprised at that comment. It convinced him that Evie's main issue had been with Angela herself and not work assignments.

He calmly said, "Evie, what is your choice?"

"I'm leaving. There's no way I'm going to be demoted to an entry level employee," she shouted.

George picked up a box.

"Very well," Michael said. "Come with us."

George and Michael led Evie up the stairs to her department. They watched as she angrily threw her personal items into the box. George took Evie's name badge and keys then walked her down the stairs and out the door.

Michael looked at Blake who had been watching.

He went over, extended his hand and said, "Blake Johnson? I'm Michael Jamison. It's nice to meet you. George is very complimentary of your work."

"It's nice to meet you, Mr. Jamison," Blake said.

"Everyone calls me Michael," he said. "Congratulations, Blake, you are now the manager of the M & L Toy Company Marketing Department, if you will take the position."

Blake smiled, "I'll be glad to take that position on one condition."

"What's that?" Michael asked.

"That I am allowed to rehire Angela Sutton," he said.

Michael smiled. "If you can get her back, you have my blessings to do so. I'm going to let you know, though, that George and I have tried to contact her, and she's not returning calls. I even went to see her personally. She's very upset, and I don't blame her. She was unfairly treated by

Evie. If you can talk her into coming back to work, I would be grateful."

Michael continued, "You have two new employees in orientation today. You can put them to work tomorrow. Go through Evie's files. Anything you don't understand or if something doesn't make sense, call me. I'll be glad to meet with you and let you know the primary sources and timings we use to advertise."

"Thank you, Michael. I'll get started on that," Blake said.

"Thank you," Michael said. "I appreciate your willingness to move into the position and to try to get Angela Sutton back in this office." Michael left the room.

*****

Xada watched Evie Barone being escorted from the building. This was not good. Out of all the employees, she was the one most receptive to his demons' suggestions. Baal was not going to be happy.

*****

Michael went back to George's office. "OK, George, call Jeffrey in."

A few minutes later, Jeffrey Wagner knocked on George's door.

"Come in, Jeffrey," George said.

Jeffrey came in and saw Michael standing beside the desk. Jeffrey looked confused.

Michael extended his hand and said, "Jeffrey, I'm Michael Jamison. I don't believe we've met."

Jeffrey shook Michael's hand. "No, Sir. It's good to meet you."

George motioned for both of them to have a seat.

Michael said, "Jeffrey, I've been looking over the complaint you filed against Sheila Davenport. Would you like to tell me about it?"

Jeffrey told Michael about his being assigned to the toys and games that were Christian in nature. He asked to be reassigned. Sheila did, but he didn't like the fact that she had assigned him there in the first place or that the company was even producing that kind of material. He said to make him work in that area was to force those beliefs on him.

Michael asked, "Did Sheila say that you had to believe in Christianity to work here?"

"No," Jeffrey answered.

"And Sheila reassigned you with no questions asked?"

Jeffrey answered, "Yes."

"Jeffrey," Michael said, "It appears to me that Sheila followed our policy about an employee's request to be reassigned to a different product in your department. She did not force you to stay on a product you didn't want to work on, nor did she try to make you believe in Christianity. I have the reports of some other employees who witnessed your conversation that will corroborate my opinion."

Michael continued, "You have a great skill set, and I would like for you to stay with the company. However, if you feel like you cannot work here because of your own personal beliefs, then I will understand if you choose to resign."

Jeffrey suddenly looked unsure. "You want me to resign?"

"No, that's not what I said," Michael answered. "I would like for you to stay, but I don't want strife in the department. I don't intend to fire Sheila Davenport because I have no evidence that she has broken company policy. This company has a history of hiring all races, religions, and ethnicities, and everyone has gotten along until now. If you feel you can't work here, we will accept your resignation with regret. If you want to stay with the company, I suggest you accept the fact that we have a product line that appeals to the Christian population in the country. It's profitable, and we will continue it. Now, what is your decision?"

Jeffrey looked at Michael then at George. He had not anticipated this turn of events, and he was no longer confident in his opinions.

"This is a good job," Jeffrey said. "I'll stay, and I'll withdraw my complaint against Sheila. As long as I don't have to work in the Christian product line, things will be fine."

"I will make sure Sheila has that information," Michael said. "I'm glad you're staying." Michael shook Jeffrey's hand and left the office.

Back in his own chair, Michael breathed a sigh of relief. He thanked God for his wisdom and protection during what had to have been a spiritual battle within his company. Then he picked up his phone and called Eleanor.

"Michael?" she answered. "Did everything go well?"

"Yes, Mom. It's over, and things feel less oppressive around here. Thank you for your prayers," he said.

"I'm glad I could help," she said. "Call any time, but I'm going to hang up and go get food."

"Go get some comfort food," Michael said. "Love you, Mom."

"Love you, too, Michael," she said and ended the call.

*****

Xada watched from a distance. He was angry. That praying woman had helped Michael turn everything into a positive. He had lost control of the strife. Baal was going to be angry.

*****

Helen tapped on Michael's door.

"Yes?" he asked.

"Did you hear what happened in the lobby?" she asked.

"No, what happened?" Michael asked.

"Millie called me. A while ago, a breeze blew the front door open and blew all the plants over. She said it was a freak wind, and a little creepy," Helen told him.

"What time did that happen?" he asked.

"Shortly before nine."

"Interesting," Michael said. "Does she need any help getting things cleaned up?"

"No. It's done," Helen said.

"Thanks for telling me," Michael said. He sat back in his chair. That was about the time he and Eleanor had started to pray. Creepy was right, but it was also reassuring that those prayers were strong enough to remove evil from the building.

*****

Eleanor walked into the kitchen where Max and Louis were eating breakfast.

She sat down and said, "We need to get back to Charlotte. Michael is in a battle for his employees and the company."

"What happened?" Louis asked.

"Your buddy, Baal, has caused all sorts of strife and conflicts within the company. There never used to be anything like that. Michael called me early to ask for prayer as he dealt with the issues. He just called back and said everything had gone well." Eleanor looked at her brothers, "Another battle. Prayer 3, Baal 0."

CHAPTER 18

The weather forecast predicted several days with no rain. Angela was mowing grass in the hay fields. She was halfway through the task when her phone rang. She looked over and didn't recognize the number. Voice mail could take that call.

When the grass was cut, Angela drove the tractor back to the equipment shed. When she came out of the building, she could smell the sweet aroma of freshly mown hay. Taking a deep breath, Angela felt content for the first time in a week. Everything seemed to be calling her to the farm and to work with her father. Angela took her phone and listened to the voice mail.

"Angela, this is Blake Johnson. I got your number from George in HR. A lot has happened here today. Evie chose to resign over being demoted to entry level. Then I got promoted to department manager. Will you come back to work? I have Michael's blessings to rehire you if you're willing. I need a seasoned professional to help run this place. It's a disaster. Evie had no idea what she was doing. You deserve to be here, and selfishly, I don't want to do this job without you. Please call me back and say you'll be here tomorrow morning."

Angela stood still in surprise, not knowing how to feel. Part of her wanted to say there was no way she would go back to work at M & L Toys. Another part of her was willing to try the job again since Evie was gone, and a small part of her had no idea what to do.

Going back to the house, Angela entered the kitchen to find both Ray and Brenda getting ready to have lunch.

She got a soft drink and sat at the table. "I need advice."

"Okay," Ray said. "Yes."

Angela laughed, "How do you know what I'm getting ready to tell you?"

Ray grinned, "You laughed. That's a good

start."

"I got a call from Blake Johnson," Angela said, still smiling. "He and I oriented together at M & L. Evie got demoted today, then she resigned. Blake is now the manager of the department. He called and said he wants me to come back to work."

"How do you feel about that?" Brenda asked.

"I don't know," Angela replied. "I'm surprised I haven't refused without a thought, but I wouldn't mind working for Blake. He's great. I'm relieved that Evie isn't there. It would have been an automatic no if she were still there, in any capacity. She was the main problem. Now that she isn't there, I feel better."

"Maybe you should try it," Ray said. "You can always resign on your own terms." He smiled, "The farm will still be here."

Angela smiled, "I liked the idea of going into business with you, Dad. It was beginning to grow on me."

"You can still help in the busy seasons," Ray said. "I'm afraid if you don't try marketing again, you'll regret it."

Angela nodded. "You're probably right." She looked at her parents and said, "Thank you for your advice and support. I think I'll call Blake. I may be going back to work tomorrow, Dad, so if there is something else you need me to do, better tell me now so I can do it this afternoon."

Ray smiled, "We're all caught up. I can bale the hay in a couple of days. Go call your new boss."

Angela went to her bedroom then tapped the call back button on the voicemail.

She heard, "This is Blake Johnson."

"Hello, Blake. This is Angela."

Blake smiled, "I can't believe you called me back! This is great. Word is you've been letting everything go to voicemail and not responding to anyone. Will you come back to work tomorrow? Angela, I need you."

"OK. I'll be there," Angela said. "If it had been anyone but you, I would've ignored the call. I think I'll like working for you, Blake."

"Hallelujah!" Blake exclaimed. "Thank you. You wouldn't want to come in this afternoon, would you?"

Angela laughed, "Don't press your luck. I'm committed to helping my dad this afternoon. I'll be back tomorrow."

"OK, then. I'll go get your ID badge from George. It'll be up here tomorrow. We have some nice kids starting, but they don't know anything," Blake said. "We'll be doing double duty while we train them."

"I like a challenge," Angela said smiling. "I'll see you in the morning." She ended the call and pondered her decision. After talking with Blake, she felt good about giving the job another try.

*****

When the call ended, Blake immediately went to George Martinez's office. He knocked on the door.

George looked up and said, "Blake, come in. Can I help you with anything?"

"Yes," Blake said. "I need Angela Sutton's ID badge. I sweet talked her into coming back to work. She'll be in tomorrow."

"That's great," George said.

"That's what I think, too," Blake said, "but I want her promoted to something above entry level. Those two you're orienting today are green and know nothing. Angela will be senior to them and tasked with training them while still doing her job."

George said, "I think that's fair. I'll bump her up a pay grade," he said as he handed the badge to Blake. "I'm glad you convinced her."

Blake smiled, "Me too!"

When Blake left his office, George immediately called Michael.

"Yes, George," Michael said.

"Good news," George said. "Blake Johnson talked Angela Sutton into coming back to work. She'll be back tomorrow."

Michael smiled and gave a sigh of relief. "Good."

George said, "Blake wants to give her a higher pay grade. She'll be senior to the guys orienting today, and Blake said they know nothing."

"Bump her up two grades. We owe her that much. She'll be working and teaching. Thanks, George," and Michael ended the call.

Michael sat at his desk thinking about staff and wondered why there weren't more applicants with experience, especially in the marketing department. As soon as he asked himself the question, Michael felt that he knew the answer. But the question was, why was his company a target for spiritual warfare? What was so unique about this company that it was brought to the attention of evil? That was a question for Mom.

*****

That evening at home, Michael changed his clothes and fell back onto his couch. What a day. He hoped he would never have another one like this. He picked up his phone and called Eleanor who was still in California.

"Michael, are you okay?" Eleanor asked. "Please tell me this is a nice chat and not another problem at the company."

"I don't know, Mom. I have a question," he said.

"What?" she asked.

"I definitely believe that the strife in the office was spiritual warfare," he said. "Right after we started praying, the front door blew open and every plant in the lobby was turned over."

"Oh, my," she said. "That's evidence of anger. We made someone angry."

"But I just realized, that with all the ads we're placing for personnel, either no one is applying or the ones applying have no experience. Is that an attack, too?" he asked.

"Could be," Eleanor said. "Historically we've had hundreds of applications for a job vacancy. I would say that you're probably right in your assumption."

"I don't know why, Mom. What about this toy company has caught the attention of evil?"

"That's a good question," Eleanor said. "I hope we get some answers before you or the company get hurt." Even though she knew the answer to the question, she was not yet in a position to tell Michael everything.

"How do I deal with this?" he asked.

"The only way you can. Prayer," Eleanor said.

"That's what I thought," he said. "Thanks, Mom. When are you guys coming back?"

"The movers are coming soon then we'll drive out. We're paying cash for the new house, so the closing will be as soon as the deeds can be searched and the place inspected," she said. "I'm looking forward to the relocation. I liked the area when we were there last week. When do we get to meet Angela?"

"I hope soon," Michael answered. "She's not very happy with me or the company right now, and I don't blame her. But she's coming back to work, so that's a good sign."

"I agree. Gotta go. I have something cooking on the stove. Love you, Son."

"Love you, too, Mom."

*****

Xada frowned. "No, it's not a good sign," he said in a disgusted cartoon voice. It's a bad sign. Angela Sutton is a praying woman. He got rid of our most receptive human and replaced her with a woman who prays. Disgusting.

Xada decided he wasn't going back to Washington. He would avoid Baal. There was no way he wanted Baal's anger to be directed at him.

CHAPTER 19

Tuesday morning, Angela dressed in her most professional outfit and drove to work. In the parking lot, she prayed for peace, creativity, and guidance in doing the right thing. As she got out of her car, Angela felt the sense of calmness that prayer always gave her.

*****

Watching Angela from a distance, a normally calm Xada threw a frustrated tantrum. Why do these people have to constantly pray? Why can't they let their guard down and ignore The Creator altogether? It would make things so much easier for him, and it would save him from Baal's anger.

*****

Angela walked down the hall of the third floor and took a deep breath before she opened the door to the marketing offices. She walked in and found Blake, who gave her a large smile and held up her name badge.

"I am so glad you're here," he said. "Close the door and have a seat." She did.

"I'm extremely relieved that Evie's gone," Blake said. "She missed getting the ad we created to all the papers in time for the sale. I think that's one reason she got demoted, plus she tried to shift blame to you and me for that. Honestly, I was glad when I watched her box up her belongings. Then I was shocked when Michael asked me to be the new manager, but my one request was that I could rehire you, so thank you for coming back to work."

Angela smiled, "It feels good to be back. Thank you."

Blake and Angela discussed the requirements of upcoming sales and events. They divided part of the tasks between them, and some they chose to work on together. The new employees, Jason and Brett, were nice guys and were eager to learn. Blake gave them some beginning tasks. As the day wore on, Angela settled in and decided she was glad she had returned to the company.

*****

Michael knew Angela was in the building. It took every ounce of willpower he had not to go down the hall and check on things. Give her space, he said to himself over and over. He needed to clear his mind to concentrate on the reports he was getting from the different departments. Coffee. He needed coffee. Taking the stairs, Michael came out on the first floor at the lobby.

Michael opened the door to the lounge and jumped back, startled.

"I'm so sorry!" he exclaimed. "I didn't expect anyone to be in here. Did I make you spill your drink?"

Angela laughed, "No. I didn't spill it, and besides, it's just ice water.

"Good," he said smiling. "I'm so glad you came back. Blake is ecstatic."

Angela nodded, "It was the right thing to do. I would have always wondered and regretted it if I hadn't."

Michael poured himself a cup of coffee.

"Are you going back upstairs?" he asked.

"Yes. Blake has me quite busy," she answered smiling.

"I'll ride the elevator with you," he said. They walked out of the lounge and into the lobby to the elevators. "What does Blake have you working on?"

"He has the new guys working on social media ads, and he has me laying out a timeline for submitting printed ads for upcoming sales. We don't want another low profit week," she said.

When the elevator doors closed, Michael smiled. "Was that professional enough in front of Millie?"

"I think so," Angela said grinning.

Michael held her hand, "I'm very glad you're back. It's been all I could do to keep from walking down the hall and check on your department."

Angela laughed. "Don't. You'll distract me."

"Then I should because I can't concentrate on anything but the fact that you're down the hall," he said with a moan.

The door opened, and they were on the third floor. "Have a nice day, Angela," he said.

"You, too, Michael," she replied.

*****

Xada mimicked their words in a sarcastic tone, "Glad you're back, Angela. Have a nice day, Angela."

He yelled, "How about go back home, Angela!"

The normally calm Xada yelled so loud the

lights blinked. Michael looked up and frowned. Plants, now the lights? He felt a chill down his spine and knew that something evil was present. He said a prayer asking for protection and commanding the demons to leave the building. Michael still didn't understand why his company was under such an intense spiritual attack. He'd never seen or felt anything like this, and he was becoming more worried.

*****

In California, Max, Louis, and Eleanor were discussing their move during breakfast.

Louis said, "I think we should sell the cars and get one large SUV for the trip back east. We can buy new vehicles there. I feel it will be safer if we are all in one car together."

"Good idea," Eleanor said. "I know it will be safer." She looked at her brothers, "It's time to tell Michael. The company is under attack. Baal is angry that you gave it to a Christian; you said so yourselves. Michael needs to understand what's happening."

"Will you tell him?" Max asked. "Baal will know if we do. Then he will really be mad."

"Alright. As soon as we're in Charlotte, I will

tell Michael everything," Eleanor said.

"You had better pray all the way there," Louis said. "If Baal discovers your intentions, he will attack us the whole trip."

"I guess we'd better get that SUV, then," Eleanor said.

The three siblings drove to the dealership they used most, sold their cars, and bought one large SUV.

CHAPTER 20

Early Monday morning, the moving company was at the Niche's house loading everything but what was packed in the SUV. When the moving van left, the house was empty.

"The realtor has a key. She'll get the place cleaned and put on the market," Louis said. "All we have left is the long trip back to Charlotte."

Eleanor looked at her brothers, "You do realize that we'll have to take turns driving and not stop. The moment we stop and are in separate hotel rooms, you'll be attacked. I fought for you on the plane, but I won't know that I need to do that again if we're separated. The best we can do is a nap in the middle of the night at a truck stop."

Max and Louis agreed, so with Max driving, the three began the journey east. They drove southeast then turned onto Interstate 40 which would take them almost the whole way to Charlotte. When it was dark, Eleanor got sleepy and laid down in the back seat with her pillow and a blanket. The road was straight, the SUV rode well, and she fell asleep.

*****

Angela woke up. It was two o'clock in the morning, but she was alert. There was a heaviness in her chest, like a burden with the need to pray. It was just like the time last week when she felt like something bad was coming. Angela knelt by the bed and began once again to pray for God to protect whoever needed his help.

*****

"Wake up!"

Eleanor sat straight up in the seat. Was she dreaming? She looked around and leaned forward to check on her brothers. Louis sat in the front passenger street with his eyes open and staring into space. He looked like he was getting ready to fall asleep. Sliding over the backseat to the console, Eleanor looked at Max. He was also staring into space, but he was speeding up. Eleanor felt a shiver of cold evil.

"Oh no!" Eleanor screamed and started shaking Max. When Max didn't wake up, she reached around the driver's seat and tried to take his foot off the accelerator.

"Jesus is Lord," she cried out while she was tugging at Max's leg. "In the name of Jesus, I command Baal and his demons to leave this vehicle." In a panic, Eleanor moved the gear shift to neutral causing the transmission to jerk.

She yelled, "In the name of Jesus, I command you to leave Max and Louis. Jesus has conquered death and sin. Jesus has conquered you! Now leave!"

Max woke, startled, and immediately moved the slowing SUV to the emergency lane. Louis opened his eyes and looked around in shock. Eleanor was still leaning over the console and crying.

"What happened?" Louis asked.

"Pull over at the next exit," Eleanor told Max. Her hands were trembling, and her voice was shaky.

Max resumed driving. A mile later, he drove up a ramp, turned right and turned into the parking lot of a truck stop. He and Louis looked at Eleanor.

Eleanor was angry and frustrated with her brothers. They had initiated this whole problem with that contract.

In a furious voice, she said, "Your friend, Baal, tried to kill us. I fell asleep. Then I heard someone shout 'wake up.' When I sat up, you both were staring into space, and Max was going faster and faster. I tried to move his leg to take his foot off the accelerator, but he was too strong. I prayed as hard as I could, and you finally woke before we crashed. I'm sure I ruined the transmission when I jammed the gear shift into neutral."

She looked at the two men, "Did you see him in your trance?"

Louis, looking shocked, said, "No. I didn't know anything until I woke up."

"I saw a beautiful oasis ahead in the desert," Max said. "I was trying to get there as fast as I could. I felt it was urgent."

"That oasis was a lie," Eleanor said angrily.

Grabbing her purse, she said, "I'm going to the restroom and then get some caffeine. It looks like I'll be driving all the way to Charlotte."

Inside the restroom, Eleanor leaned against the wall. She was scared. She was so scared that she was shaking and crying.

"Oh Lord," she prayed, "I know you woke me. Thank you. I don't know what to do. This is overwhelming and frightening. I'm so scared.

Please keep us safe until we can get to Charlotte. Please help me convince Max and Louis that they can still accept you as their Savior."

Walking back to the car and knowing that prayer had saved her life, Eleanor whispered, "Prayer 4, Baal 0."

*****

Xada watched as Eleanor regained control of the car and the entire situation. He was angry. He had planned to crash the car and kill Eleanor, but something woke her. He could tell by her aura that someone had been praying for her which strengthened her prayers. He had to find out who that was.

*****

Shortly after midnight on Wednesday morning, Eleanor was exhausted. Since she took over the driving, she had only slept three hours at a truck stop the night before. It was one in the morning, and she pulled into the parking lot of another truck stop that was open all night. Max got out and filled the gas tank. When he was back in the car, Eleanor drove to a parking place on the far end of the store, leaned her head back and fell asleep.

"Do you think she'll make it?" Max asked.

"Yes. She's a strong woman," Louis said, "but

we need to stay awake while she sleeps."

*****

Angela was sleeping peacefully when suddenly, at two o'clock in the morning, she woke up. She had that same burdening need to pray as she had the night before. Something was wrong somewhere. Throwing back the covers, Angela knelt beside the bed and began to pray for the safety and wellbeing of whoever needed it.

*****

It was still dark when the Niche siblings resumed their trip. Eleanor was trying to stay within the speed limit, but it was so tempting to speed and get to Charlotte quicker. She was driving slightly over the speed limit when a blue light started flashing behind her. Eleanor sighed with frustration. This was just great. What else was going to happen?

Eleanor pulled over and got her license and the registration. A highway patrolman walked to the driver's door. Eleanor pushed the button to lower the window. She looked up. The man looked back at her with yellow glowing eyes. She screamed. She looked at Max and Louis. They looked back at her with the same yellow, glowing eyes. Eleanor screamed again.

Eleanor heard, "Wake up," and she was instantly awake and looking around the SUV.

*****

Xada was giddy. The woman was tired, and she had fallen asleep without praying. He hovered over the car. Grinning, he eased through the roof and onto the front seat. He began to stroke Eleanor's hair then entered her dream. Just as he was about to terrify her, a veil of protection appeared in front of Eleanor, and he couldn't reach her.

He screamed in frustration and left the car. He watched from a distance as the woman became wide awake and resumed their journey. Xada was so angry that he howled and screamed obscenities. Who was praying for that woman? This was the third time someone had intervened for her. He had to find out who was doing that.

*****

Eleanor inhaled a deep, sharp breath as she woke. Looking around, she saw that Max and Louis were watching her. They could tell by the scared, wide-eyed look on her face that something was wrong.

Louis frowned, "Did you have a bad dream?"

"More like your bad friend," she snarled. "I dreamed I was pulled over for speeding. The patrolman had yellow glowing eyes, and so did you two. I'm confused. Either he got past my prayers for protection, or I had a bad dream. Either way, I'm wide awake. We may as well go farther."

Finally, late Wednesday morning after almost three days of driving across the country, Eleanor pulled into the garage of their rental house in Charlotte. She was so relieved to be finished and safe that she began to cry. Eleanor said a pray of thanks and a request for protection.

Then Eleanor said, "Boys, you can unload. I'm going to bed." She walked into the house, crawled into her bed and immediately fell asleep.

As Eleanor walked into the house, Max looked at Louis, "He would have killed us if she hadn't been driving."

"No," Louis said. "He would have killed her. He won't kill us until he gets his toy company back. It's a matter of pride for him. Our giving the company to Michael represents a loss of control." Max nodded in agreement, and the two began to unload the car.

*****

Eleanor slept until three o'clock.

She found her brothers in the den and said, "I'm going to call Michael and invite him over for dinner."

With sad faces, Max and Louis nodded. They knew what Eleanor was going to tell Michael, and there was every chance that the nephew they loved would hate them.

Eleanor dialed Michael's number.

"Mom!" Michael exclaimed quietly. "Are you back?"

Eleanor said, "Yes, we got in this morning, and I took a nap. Can you come over for dinner? Max and Louis are getting takeout from the steak house. How do you like your steak?"

"Medium," Michael said. "If you're tired, why don't we wait and let you rest."

"No," Eleanor said. "I have something I need to discuss with you, and I don't want to do it over the phone."

"Is everything alright?" Michael asked, suddenly worried.

"Yes," Eleanor answered. "I didn't mean to alarm you. It would take too long, and I don't want to tie up your office phone. Just come over for dinner. Be here at six."

"Alright," Michael said. "Now I'm curious. I'll see you at six."

Chapter 21

Michael finished his day anticipating dinner with his family. He was curious as to what Eleanor wanted to discuss.

Just before six, Michael knocked on the door of the rental house. He opened it and called, "Hello! It's Michael!"

"Come on in," Eleanor called from inside the house. "We're in the kitchen."

Michael walked through the house and entered the kitchen to find Eleanor filling glasses with iced tea. Max and Louis were getting the food out of the take-out bags.

Max handed Michael several containers and said, "This is yours."

When everyone had their food, Eleanor led them to the dining room where she said a blessing and everyone began to eat. Michael noticed that Eleanor and his uncles were quiet, which was unlike his family.

Michael looked at the three of them and said, "You guys look exhausted. Did you not stop to rest on the trip?"

Eleanor shook her head no, "We drove straight through. We were in a hurry to get here. We close on the house Monday, and the furniture will be here two days after that. There's just a lot to get done."

Louis looked at Michael and said, "Tell us about the company. Eleanor said you've been having a bit of drama."

Michael nodded and told them about what had happened in the product development department with an employee not wanting to work on any merchandise related to Christianity. He also told them about the problems in the marketing department and how Evie had quit after being demoted.

Michael looked at Max and Louis, "We never had that kind of drama when you two owned the company. Maybe you made a mistake passing it down to me so soon."

Louis shook his head, "No. Giving you the company was a good decision. We have no doubts about that." He and Max had finished eating.

Max and Louis looked at each other, then Louis said to Michael and Eleanor, "Excuse us, please." They quietly got up and left.

Michael gave Eleanor a confused look.

"What's going on?" Michael asked. "They never leave the table like that. In fact, all three of you seem to be bothered by something."

Eleanor pushed her plate back and said, "I need to give you some information. Most of it is about Max and Louis and the beginning of the toy company. They didn't want to be in the room while we talked."

Michael frowned. "This sounds bad."

"It is," Eleanor said. "I don't know all the details, because they haven't told me everything. They started the company several years before you were born. They were young, idealistic, and had big dreams. They were impatient to succeed, and they made a lot of mistakes. They were just about to go bankrupt and lose the company when they were approached by a businessman who offered to help them. In return, they had to promise to join and support his organization. He handed them a contract and gave them 24 hours to read it and think about it.

"Louis read it thoroughly, page after page, every single word. Through all the legal words and phrases, they finally discovered the truth of the contract. The businessman was a member of Satan's church. He was a recruiter and was looking for new members. Even though they didn't believe in a church of Satan, Max and Louis were so desperate to succeed, they signed the contract. They mistakenly thought that since the businessman was human that they could eventually get out of the agreement. They were wrong.

"When the man required them to go to their first ritualistic service, they realized they were under the control and authority of Satan, Baal as he likes to be called. Right then they knew they had made a terrible mistake."

Michael looked astonished. "So, you're saying, that Max and Louis will go to hell, and they chose to do that to succeed in the toy business?"

"Exactly," Eleanor said.

"Why?" Michael asked with a look of horror. "Why would anyone do that?"

Eleanor shrugged, "I asked the same thing. They couldn't give me a good answer. I'm convinced that they were deceived by that businessman. These people call their master Baal, and Baal is known as the great deceiver.

"Anyway, I figured it out after you and I moved in with them because the two were careless with some of the literature they had. I found it. At first I was so shocked I couldn't move. It was unbelieveable. Then my heart broke. Max and Louis were raised in the Christian Church just like I was, and they had turned their backs on their faith. Anyway, they had no clue that I knew what they were into until I admitted it a few weeks ago when I told them we needed to move to Charlotte to protect you and the company."

Michael sat staring at Eleanor as she talked. He was having difficulty processing what she was saying. It seemed so implausible that the uncles he loved so much had made such a choice.

Eleanor continued, "Do you remember how we used to go for weekend trips once a month?"

"Yes," Michael said, smiling. "I was especially fond of Disneyland and then skiing."

"I enjoyed those weekends too," Eleanor said, "but those were the weekends Max and Louis had to attend some sort of ritual with that group. I didn't want you anywhere near that. I thought about moving out, but they hid it well, and you must admit, they were great role models for you."

Michael smiled, "Yes. I learned a lot of guy things from them. It was like having two fathers."

Eleanor placed her hand on Michael's hand.

"They adore you, Michael," she said. "Never forget that. You are the child they never had. When they realized what they had done, they chose to never marry. Neither one of them wanted to bring a wife or children into Baal's influence. I think the only reason they let me move in was because I was determined to raise you in the Christian faith."

"So, why did the uncles hand the company down to me early?" Michael asked.

"Max and Louis are fully aware of what they have done, and they regret it more than you could know," Eleanor said. "They didn't want Baal to have the company or to be able to influence anyone in charge of the company. The only way they knew to accomplish that was to give the company to you, a Christian." She suddenly looked sad, "They mentioned that their day of reckoning isn't far away now. They wanted to put things in place before that happens."

Michael interupted her, "Day of reckoning?

What does that mean?"

"If I understand it correctly, the day of reckoning is the term Max and Louis have given to the moment they will die, and Baal will take their souls," Eleanor said sadly.

A look of horror appeared on Michael's face. Eleanor nodded, acknowledging how Michael felt.

She took a deep breath, "Baal never bothered them before, but now he's furious with them for handing the company over to someone who loves the Lord. He has tried on several occasions to torment them, but I've been able to protect them with prayer." Eleanor sighed, "I'm getting tired. I have come between them and Baal so many times now that Baal is trying to get rid of me."

Eleanor told Michael the story about hearing someone shout wake up and finding Max speeding up.

She said, "I prayed so hard. If we had crashed, I would've been killed, but I'm sure Baal would have protected Max and Louis."

Michael could not help the look of fear and concern on his face.

"Mom, what did you do?" he asked.

"I drove all the way here," she said. "At one

point I was so tired that I parked at a truck stop for a nap. Baal got too close then, too. He entered my dream, which became like a scary nightmare. But again, a clear, loud voice told me to wake up. Michael, I think someone is praying for me, but I don't know who. It must be someone who listens to the spirit when told to pray, even when he or she doesn't know why. I truly believe God's voice woke me up and saved me twice because someone, somewhere has been faithful enough to pray."

"What do we do?" Michael asked.

"I believe that Baal realizes he may not get the company back through Max and Louis," Eleanor said. "I believe he is behind the troubles and drama at the office. If he can cause enough problems, you may lose the company or be tempted to sell."

"That explains a lot, but what do we do about Max and Louis?" Michael asked. "They obviously regret their actions, but how do we get them out of this?"

"They're convinced that because they chose Baal, that God will never forgive them," Eleanor said sadly.

"But that's not true," Michael argued. "All they have to do is repent and accept Jesus."

"I know that, and you know that. But Baal has deceived them so badly that they cannot grasp grace of that magnitude," Eleanor said.

"This is so hard to process. I feel so sad for Max and Louis and how they must be feeling," Michael said.

"I know," Eleanor said. "They're afraid to face you. That's why they left the room. They're ashamed of all of this."

Michael nodded in understanding and thanked Eleanor for revealing the truth about the company. Getting up, Michael walked into the living room and looked out the window. The sunset was beautiful and peaceful. Michael prayed for his uncles and for the wisdom to handle this issue without making Max and Louis feel even worse about the situation.

After a few minutes, Michael turned and went in search of Max and Louis. He found them on the back patio, staring into a fire pit. They looked up when he came outside. The expression on their faces was so sad to Michael. It hurt him to think about the inner turmoil they must be feeling. He wanted badly to help them and ease their distress.

Michael loved his uncles and was grateful for all the times they helped and guided him throughout his life. Now it was his turn to help them get through one of the biggest battles of their lives. Michael took a seat with them next to the fire pit.

"Mom told me everything," he said softly. "This doesn't change how I feel about the two of you. You're the only fathers I have ever known. I love you both, and that will never change." Michael saw their sadness change to relief.

"Thank you," Louis said sincerely. "We love you too. We never intended for any of this to affect you, the company, or the people you love. We especially hate that we have put Eleanor in danger."

"Regret is not a strong enough word to express how we feel about our decision," Max said sadly. "It was the biggest mistake of our lives. In hindsight, I would rather we had lost the company than be dealing with these consequences."

"I believe you," Michael said. "We can make a plan to keep Baal out of the company and to remove you from his contract."

"How?" Max asked. "We are so far under his control that we can't get anywhere near M & L Toys."

Michael smiled and shook his head, "You're breaking away from him more than you realize.

You gave the company to a Christian. If you were completely under Baal's spell, you would have never done that."

Max smiled, "You're right. I hadn't thought of it that way."

"You can get out of the contract," Michael said. "You just have to go to Christ. I know you've done that, before Baal entered your life."

"That's impossible," Louis said sadly.

"No. It isn't," Michael replied. "Have you forgotten that nothing is impossible with God? But I won't pressure you about that tonight. You're all tired."

Eleanor walked up to the fire pit and sat in one of the chairs. The four of them sat quietly, gazing into the fire. They felt the comfort of family solidarity, especially knowing there may be more battles ahead.

After a while, Michael looked at his watch. "It's getting late; I need to go." He smiled, "I want to schedule a time to bring Angela over so you can meet her. You will love her."

"I want to meet her," Eleanor said.

"We do too," Louis answered.

"Give me a few days to rest and recuperate, then I will cook dinner for us all," Eleanor said.

Michael said, "Let me know when you're

ready, and we'll arrange a good time to come over." The four stood up, and Michael hugged each one of his family members.

"I love you all," he told them. "Never forget that."

Then Michael turned and walked to his car. All the way home he could not stop thinking about what he had learned and wondered how he was going to help his uncles.

CHAPTER 22

Thursday morning, Angela blinked to focus on the list of toys scheduled to go on sale next month. She yawned again. Frustrated, Angela stood and walked to Blake's office.

"I'm going downstairs for coffee," Angela said. "I'll be right back."

"OK," Blake answered without looking up from his computer.

Angela smiled and took the stairs to the lobby. She walked into the lounge and poured herself a cup of coffee. She opened the refrigerator, took out the flavored creamer that she had brought and added it to her cup. Sitting at one of the tables, Angela sipped her coffee.

*****

Michael walked into the lobby of the building. He was late, but he had taken a call from the company's European sales manager.

Michael wanted coffee and opened the door to the lounge. He saw Angela sitting at a table drinking her coffee. She looked tired. He walked in and poured a cup of coffee then went and sat opposite her at the table.

"Are you alright?" he asked.

"Ummhmm," she muttered. "Poor sleep. Two nights in a row. That's not like me."

"Why couldn't you sleep?" he asked with concern.

Angela looked at him, "It's the strangest thing. Two nights in a row this week and one a couple weeks ago, I woke up instantly alert with the need to pray. I have no idea for whom or why. I just prayed for an unknown person's health and safety. Then, last night, I tossed and turned. I think I was nervous about it happening again."

Michael blinked in surprise. It sounded like the times Eleanor thought someone had been praying for her and wondered if Angela was that unknown person.

"And you have no idea who or why?" he asked.

"Nope. But I hope whoever it is has been safe and well," she said.

"I'm sure they are. You're a faithful prayer warrior." Michael reached across the table and traced the back of Angela's hand with his index finger.

"Would you have dinner with me tonight?" he asked.

Angela smiled, "Yes, but not too late. I have to work in the morning, and my boss is a stickler for punctuality."

"Overbearing bosses," Michael said grinning. "My family wants to meet you. They got back yesterday and are exhausted. They drove straight through without stopping for the night anywhere." Michael shook his head, "Crazy kids."

Angela giggled, "I would like to meet them. I want to meet the people who raised you and get the embarrassing stories you don't want told."

"Hey!" he said with feigned indignation. "Who says I have embarrassing stories?"

"We all have embarrassing stories," she said laughing.

The lounge door opened, and two women from the product development department came in.

"Oh," one said. "Are we interrupting? Can we get coffee?"

Michael smiled, "Come in. I just got here and stopped for coffee. Evidently Ms. Sutton had a wild night with little sleep and needed coffee."

Angela frowned, "Don't listen to him. Come and get your coffee. Are you from product development?"

"Yes," they answered.

Michael said, "Angela, this is Amber and Jennifer, two talented ladies from product development. Ladies, this is Angela, a talented member of the marketing team."

Angela said, "It's nice to meet you. Would you sit for a minute? I need to pick your brains for an ad."

Michael stood and said, "Now this is what I like, departmental collaboration. I'm going so you can get creative." Michael smiled and left the room.

When Michael left the room, Angela proceeded to ask Jennifer and Amber about the processes used in their department, trying to learn all she could from them. Thirty minutes later, Angela walked back into the marketing department.

"Did you have to make the coffee?" Blake asked grinning. Angela went into this office and closed the door.

She said, "I had a conference with some girls in product development. Let me tell you my idea."

Blake grinned as he listened to Angela's idea for a new marketing campaign. She had just started, and he was already on board with her plan. He was impressed with her creativity. When Angela had finished explaining her idea, he fully approved the campaign and was excited to move forward.

Angela was back at her desk working when Blake's phone rang. He answered, "Blake Johnson."

"Blake, this is Sheila Davenport in Product Development."

"Sheila!" Blake said, "I was going to call you."

"Good," she said, sounding annoyed. "So, you're upset with your employee, too."

"What?" Blake was shocked. "I don't think we're talking about the same thing. Why are you annoyed with one of my employees?"

"I let two girls in my department go to the lounge to get coffee," Sheila said. "What I thought would be a five-minute trip across the hall turned into a half hour. They said that Angela in marketing sat them down and started asking questions about how to implement an idea she had. Blake, any ideas for toys come from me and my senior staff or Michael, not from marketing. Also, they don't come from any of my level one employees. I would appreciate you telling your staff member to not waste my people's time and to stick to her job which is promoting toys, not developing them."

Blake was speechless for a moment, then replied, "Sheila, I'm sorry you're unhappy, but I was going to call you to discuss the idea that Angela and I have worked out for a company promotion. She didn't give your employees ideas for toys. She asked how the department worked so that she wouldn't step on your toes or interfere with your process. I'm sorry if those girls did not convey that to you."

Sheila said, "Those girls also said Michael was okay with everything."

"No," Blake said. "That's not true, either. He made a comment that he liked departmental collaboration and didn't mind their talking. He had no idea what Angela was trying to find out."

"What's with the familiarity between Michael and this girl?" Sheila asked. "My girls said when they walked into the lounge, the two were sitting at a table talking."

Blake was starting to get angry, "Sheila, where is this coming from? As far as I can tell, Angela has done no harm except making your girls take too long a break."

"I don't want to have to tip toe around the boss's girlfriend," Sheila snarled.

Blake's frustration was growing.

In a low angry tone, he said, "Sheila, don't start rumors. If they were talking, he was probably checking up on her. Angela was treated very badly her second day on the job and was wrongly fired. I wanted her back when I was made manager, so I asked Michael for permission to rehire her. Unfortunately, she wasn't taking phone calls. Michael found out where she lived and went to see her personally to apologize officially from the company and ask her to come back to work."

"Why would he do that?" she asked.

"Because Angela is that talented. Plus, she and I work well together, and I wanted her back," Blake said.

"Well, fine," Sheila said, "just keep her away from my department." Sheila ended the call abruptly.

Blake looked in shock at the quiet phone. What was going on? Angela had done nothing wrong, and he thought Sheila was out of line. He decided he wasn't going to tell Angela about the conversation, because he didn't want to risk losing her from the company again. It seemed like everyone at M & L Toys was trying hard to keep her from working here, and he didn't understand why.

*****

Xada smiled. He stroked Sheila Davenport's head, whispering venom about Angela Sutton into her ears, telling her that Angela was trying to control product development. Xada fed Sheila's anger and indignation until she had called Blake.

*****

Jennifer and Amber were quietly working at their stations. Sheila was angry with them, and they didn't want to do anything that would make her angrier. The woman didn't let them fully explain what had happened. When she heard that Angela had asked questions about the department, the woman flushed red, went into her office and slammed the door.

The girls hoped they didn't get Angela in trouble and decided to avoid Sheila as much as possible the rest of the day. They didn't want to get yelled at again.

*****

Later that afternoon, Michael took a break from his computer and rubbed his neck. He smiled when he thought about Angela's friendliness with other employees. That had to be good for the company. He decided to text her about dinner plans.

Angela's phone buzzed with a text.

Michael: Want to meet me at the restaurant or go home and have me pick you up?

Angela: I can meet you. Where?

Michael: Italian. Shopping center one exit down.

Angela: That place is great. What time?

Michael: Let's just go there from here. As soon after five as you can get there. I'll have a table.

Angela: OK. Can't wait.

Chapter 23

Amber looked at her watch. Finally, it was five o'clock.

She said to Jennifer, "This has been a long day. I'm starving. Want to get an early dinner and unwind?"

"Sure," Jennifer said. "Where?"

"I know a great place. Follow me," Amber said as they walked to the parking lot.

*****

Xada grinned. He stroked Amber's head with his dark, sharply curved nails.

In a hissing and gruff voice, he whispered, "Italian."

*****

Angela closed her laptop, got her purse and waved to Blake as she went out the door. Something was bothering Blake, but she didn't want to intrude by asking about it. She had a lot of respect for Blake and hoped that he was okay.

Getting into her car, Angela settled into the driver's seat and checked her hair in the rearview mirror. She smiled as she pulled out of the parking lot and drove to meet Michael at the restaurant.

*****

Michael walked into the restaurant. The aroma of Italian food was strong and made his stomach growl. The interior was long and narrow with booths along each side of the aisle, and the atmosphere was relaxed and quiet. He asked the hostess for a table and was seated at a booth in the back.

The waitress brought two menus and two waters. When she left the table, Michael looked up to see Angela walking in. He felt like his heart skipped a beat, and he couldn't help the smile that appeared on his face as soon as he saw her.

Michael stood and motioned her over to their table. When she got there, he gave her a hug and asked, "Hungry?"

"Starving," she said. "I skimped on lunch. This is a great idea. I'm really glad you asked me to dinner. Food and your company. What could be better?"

Michael smiled, "I could say the same thing."

*****

Out in the parking lot, Amber and Jennifer exited their cars and walked together into the restaurant. The hostess seated them at a booth in the front on the opposite side of the restaurant from Michael and Angela.

Jennifer looked around the restaurant.

"This is a nice place, and it smells amazing. I'm ready for some good comfort food after the day we've had." She paused, "Oh my gosh," she said looking at the back of the room.

"What?" Amber asked.

"Michael Jamison is sitting in a booth in the back," Jennifer said.

"I guess he likes this place, too," Amber replied.

"He's with a woman!" Jennifer whispered.

Amber's eyes got big. "No way! Can you see her? What does she look like?"

"I can't see her," Jennifer said. "Her back is to us, and the booth hides her."

"Then how do you know it's a woman?" Amber asked.

"I saw a leg and very feminine sandals," Jennifer said. "That is not a man."

Amber grinned and said, "Eat slow. Maybe

they'll finish first and leave so we can see her."

*****

"How was your day?" Michael asked.

"Good," Angela answered. "Blake and I are working on a holiday promotion."

"What is it?" Michael asked.

"It isn't finished,'" Angela said. "Besides, it's up to Blake to pitch the idea to you, and I'm not going to steal his thunder."

Michael smiled, "Alright. I'll be patient, and that's very thoughtful of you. You're going to make your boss look good, aren't you?"

"It's a team effort, but I hope so. He's a great boss," she said. "How was last night with your family? Were your mother and uncles exhausted from their trip?"

"Yes," Michael said. "Mom drove almost the whole way and only stopped for small naps. They were in a hurry to get here. By the way, you're invited to dinner at their house Monday night."

"Aren't you going, too?" Angela asked trying not to laugh.

Michael rolled his eyes, "Yes, I will be there too, smart aleck."

Angela laughed. Michael loved that sound. "Mom in particular wants to meet you."

"I would like to meet her and your uncles," Angela said.

"I hope you like them as much as I like your parents," he said.

"I'm sure I will. I like you, so it can't be too much of a stretch to like your family, too," Angela told him as she grinned.

The waitress brought their orders. They paused their conversation to say a blessing and began to eat.

*****

"Oh!" Jennifer said.

"What?" Amber asked.

"The waitress just brought Michael and the mystery woman their food. They held hands and had a blessing. I guess our big boss is a Christian. That's nice," Jennifer told her.

"That's no big deal," Amber said. "Half the people in this state are Christians."

"Yes," Jennifer said. "But he's from California."

Amber rolled her eyes, "Jennifer, there are Christians there, too."

"Don't get testy," Jennifer said, sounding slightly annoyed. "I just said that I thought it was nice."

*****

Michael and Angela had finished their meal,

and Michael ordered one dessert with two forks. Angela excused herself and made a trip to the restroom.

When she came back to the booth, she said, "We may have a problem. Those two girls I talked with from product development, Amber and Jennifer, are sitting at a booth near the front. They have a direct line of vision to you, and they just saw me leave and come back."

"Why is that a problem?" Michael asked.

"Rumors will run rampant all over the company," Angela said. "I don't want it to cause you a problem."

"What about you?" he asked. "Won't it cause you problems with your coworkers?"

"Not if they don't hear about it. If they do, I'll just explain that we knew each other when I lived in Durham, that you had no influence on my being hired and that you didn't even know I had been hired to work for the company until you saw my name on a memo from George," she said.

Michael smiled, "Well, that is true except for one thing."

"What?" she asked.

He paused, looked into Angela's eyes and sincerely said, "I know exactly who you are and what I'm doing. I intend to be more than just friends with you, Angela. Get used to the idea." He took her left hand and tapped her ring finger.

"Let me make my intentions clear. I'm a patient man, and I don't want to scare you away, but I already have deep feelings for you. I predict that this time next year, you'll be wearing an engagement ring from me. That's how fast I have been falling for you since we met on that plane."

Angela blinked with astonishment. She felt her pulse quicken and butterflies race through her stomach. Every feeling she had been developing for Michael just revved up into high gear. Angela was shocked and excited all at the same time and was glad that her feelings were returned.

Taking a deep breath, Angela smiled and asked, "That's your prediction?"

"Absolutely," Michael said emphatically.

Angela smiled, "I hope your prediction comes true, then." Their eyes locked. Their gaze lingered in understanding that they felt the same way about each other.

Michael leaned forward, "Do you know how much I want to kiss you right now?"

"Probably about as much as I would like to kiss you, but remember, you're a patient man," Angela reminded him.

Michael burst into laughter. Everyone on their end of the restaurant turned to look.

"Turning my words around on me?" Michael asked. "Well, I don't care as long as the outcome is you wearing my ring."

*****

"Well, something sure was funny," Jennifer said. "I've never seen Michael Jamison laugh that hard, ever."

"You rarely see the man," Amber reminded her. "He could be a clown for all we know."

Jennifer rolled her eyes at Amber and took another bite of food.

*****

Michael paid the bill.

As he and Angela slipped out of their seats, Michael whispered, "Guess it's time to go back to being best friends in front of the employees." Angela gave him an understanding smile as they walked toward the door.

Angela stopped at the table and said, "Hey Jennifer; hey Amber. This is a great place to eat, isn't it."

Before Jennifer or Amber could answer,

Michael said, "Thanks for the company, Angela. I'll see you tomorrow."

Angela laughed, "No you won't."

"Why," Michael asked.

"Because the big dogs don't play with the puppies," Angela said, giving Michael a knowing look.

Michael laughed. "And just who are you calling a puppy?"

Angela rolled her eyes, "Go on." She sat beside Amber. "I'm going to talk with my girls here." Michael laughed and turned to leave. Angela called out, "Thanks for dinner!"

Michael gave her a thumbs up and left the restaurant.

Angela chuckled then turned to Jennifer and Amber who were staring at her with their mouths open.

"What?" Angela asked.

"Why were you having dinner with Michael Jamison?" Amber asked.

Angela shrugged. "Michael and I met while I was still living and working in Durham. I had no idea he owned M & L Toys, and he didn't know that I was hired for a job there. He knew I thought of him as just Michael and not a CEO. Anyway, he drove to Durham, took me to dinner, and confessed that he owned the company. I told him I didn't care if he owned the company. I wanted that job. Anyway, we're friends. My boss is Blake, and I never see Michael at the office."

"What about the employee lounge this morning?" Jennifer asked.

"Oh, that was sheer coincidence," Angela said. "I was sleepy and needed coffee. He was coming in late and wanted coffee. We sat down and played catch up for a few minutes. That's all."

"Did you know we got into trouble for talking with you so long this morning?" Amber asked.

Angela looked shocked, "No! What happened?"

"Sheila, our boss, was mad that we didn't come back in five minutes," Jennifer said. "We told her we were answering your questions and why. She went ballistic. I think she called your boss and complained."

"I'm so sorry! I never meant for that to happen!" Angela exclaimed. She looked confused, "Blake didn't say anything to me about that. I'll ask him tomorrow. Didn't you tell her that Michael was in the room and joked about liking departmental collaboration?"

"Yes," Amber said, "and that made her even

madder. I honestly think she was mad that we had been at the right place at the right time to run into him and make a positive impression. I think she was jealous."

"I'm so sorry," Angela said. "I never dreamed you would get into trouble. Is she controlling?"

"Not bad," Amber said. "I think she gets under a lot of pressure to develop new toys for the holidays. They need to be in production, ready and shipped by July to get on the store shelves in time for Christmas shopping."

"Huh," Angela said. "I can see how that would be a stressor. We're already planning holiday promotions for the toys being produced."

Angela stood, "I need to get home. I still have horses and chickens to feed. Maybe I'll see you at the office, but I promise I'll only say hello. I'm really sorry if I caused any problems for y'all."

"No worries," Jennifer said. "Everything will be alright."

Amber nodded and said, "See you later."

When Angela left the restaurant, Amber looked at Jennifer and asked, "Do you believe her story?"

"I mean, maybe? It's plausible. I don't think we should start a rumor, though," Jennifer answered.

"Yeah, you're right. Michael would know where it came from, and we would really be in trouble then," Amber replied.

*****

Xada was getting angry. He kept trying to get Jennifer to start the rumor. He wanted employees to get angry and suspicious of Angela so she would have to leave the company and get out of Michael's life. But for some reason, the woman was resistant. At least her hesitance to start a rumor was self preservation and not a noble gesture.

Chapter 24

Friday morning, Angela knocked on Blake's office door. "Good morning!" he said. "What can I do for you?"

Angela entered his office and closed the door. "Did you get a complaint about me yesterday?"

"Yes, and how did you know?" he asked.

"I ran into Jennifer and Amber at a restaurant last night. They're the girls I talked with from product development. They told me that they got into trouble for talking with me, and that Sheila called you to complain," Angela told him. "Is everything okay? I didn't mean to cause any problems for you."

"Yes, Sheila called me," he said. "I didn't say anything to you because I thought she was out of line. I thought she was overreacting and trying to pull rank. I really like the idea, and

I intend to present it at the next staff meeting when Michael meets with department managers. Please don't worry. You're an amazing employee, and you've done nothing wrong."

"Thanks for saying that," Angela replied, "but there's something else."

"What?" he asked, looking concerned.

"I was having dinner at the restaurant with Michael. Just so you know, we knew each other before I came to work here. I had no idea he was the Michael Jamison of M & L Toys. He had no idea I had been hired until he got my name on the list of employees from George. I imagine your name was on the same list since we oriented together. Michael jokes that I'm his only friend in North Carolina, and he was tired of eating alone. Nothing to it. We're friends, but he's not my direct boss, so I see nothing wrong with it, and neither does he. We don't run in the same circles at the office. I'm way too low on the food chain," she said grinning.

Blake looked at her and asked, "If you're friends, why didn't you pull the friend card and get the manager's position in this department?"

Angela answered sincerely, "Blake, you have more experience than I do. Plus, you're great at management. I've only been a one man show.

I have no idea how to manage people. You were perfect for the job, and I like working for you. I think things worked out as they should have. I have no intention of bypassing the chain of command just because I'm friends with Michael. I don't operate that way." She stood and grinned, "I just wanted to clear the air and make sure you're okay. I need to get back to work. My bosses are very demanding."

Blake smiled, "Thanks for telling me, Angela. And for the record, I wouldn't care if you were married to the man. We make a great team, and I would want to continue that." Angela smiled and left his office.

Angela stayed busy creating designs for the new ad compaign that Blake had approved. She wanted to make sure everything was ready by the time he would present it for approval at the next managers' meeting, and she had made a lot of progress by the end of the day.

*****

Monday morning, Angela was trying to concentrate on her work. She had seen Michael over the weekend, and her thoughts kept going back to their time together. Suddenly, she felt her cell phone buzz with a text. It was from Michael.

Michael: Just reminding you about dinner tonight with me and my family.

Angela: I remember.

Michael: I have to work a little overtime. Why don't you go home, and I'll pick you up there. Mom knows I'll be a little late.

Angela: OK. How late is a little overtime? Do we need to reschedule?

Michael: No. Mom would kill me. She really wants to meet you. I'll be at your house no later than six, I hope.

Angela: Sounds good. See you then.

*****

Angela was excited to spend more time with Michael. It had been a busy day, and she couldn't think of anything better than being near him. She liked the way she relaxed around him.

Having changed from her professional clothes to a more casual dress and shoes, Angela saw Michael driving up to the house. She smiled, grabbed her purse and a sweater and went downstairs. Looking into the kitchen, Angela gave Brenda a quick goodbye before walking out onto the porch to greet Michael.

Angela gave him a warm hug and said, "Hi. I'm ready."

"Did you get your work done?" Angela asked once they were in the car.

"I did," Michael said. "Now I can enjoy the evening without worrying about it."

"Good," Angela said smiling. They talked during the entire ride, mostly about their day. Before long Michael was parking at a house in Huntersville.

"This is their rental house, which came furnished. They closed on their new house today and their furniture will be here in another two or three days," Michael told her.

He got out of the car and opened the passenger door for Angela. She admired the front porch furniture as Michael rang the doorbell and opened the door.

"Mom!" he called.

Eleanor came out of the kitchen, wiping her hands on her apron. She walked over to Michael and gave him a hug, "Hello, Michael."

"Mom," Michael said smiling. "This is Angela Sutton. Angela, this is my mother, Eleanor Jamison."

Eleanor smiled and took Angela's hands, "I'm so happy to meet you."

"I'm excited to meet you, too," Angela said.

Two men came from the back of the house into the living room.

Michael said, "Angela, these are the uncles, Max and Louis Niche."

Max came over, took Angela's hand and said, "I'm Max. It's great to meet you."

Louis bumped Max to the side and said, "I'm Louis. Welcome."

Angela smiled and said, "This is wonderful. I'm so excited to meet you all."

"Come into the dining room,' Eleanor said. "Dinner is ready."

Angela sat at the table with Michael and his family. Not only was the food delicious, but she laughed so much her cheeks were beginning to hurt. The conversation was animated, and she could tell this was a close, loving family.

*****

Xada decided it was time to check in on Max and Louis. He had left them alone too long. When he got to their house, he looked inside. The family was at the dinner table, and there was a guest.

"NOOO!" Xada screamed. "Those two praying

women are in the same house!"

The praying woman, Eleanor, had managed to get a hedge of protection around the house. He couldn't get close enough to hear the conversation, but he didn't want those two women together. Xada was furious. He shouted obscenities and made the sky grow dark. A fierce straight-line wind blew through the neighborhood, pushing trees over and breaking limbs. Large limbs fell in the yard of the rental house.

Alarmed at the sound of the wind, Eleanor looked outside. She could feel the cold evil as it sent shivers up her spine to her neck. She turned to Max and Louis. They sat completely frozen with fear. They knew this was not a typical weather event. Baal or someone else was outside, and he was not happy.

"Excuse me," Eleanor said. She ran into the living room, dropped to her knees by the couch and immediately began to pray.

Angela watched Eleanor run into the next room. She looked at Max and Louis who looked terrified. Looking at Michael, she could see his confused expression turning into understanding.

Suddenly, Angela felt burdened with the need to pray. The need was so strong she turned to

Michael and grabbed his hand.

"I need to pray!" she whispered.

Michael nodded in agreement and pointed to the living room, "We'll go in there."

Michael and Angela hurried into the living room. They saw Eleanor praying out loud. The two held hands and knelt beside Eleanor. All three prayed aloud for God to protect them against all evil and to calm the storm. Soon, the wind stopped blowing, and the cold force of evil had vanished.

Eleanor looked at Angela, "It was you, wasn't it? You're the one who's been praying for me."

Angela looked shocked, "Are you the one who needed my prayers in the middle of the night?"

"Yes," Eleanor said, tears welling in her eyes. "You actually saved my life." Eleanor hugged Angela. "Thank you."

Angela hugged Eleanor in return.

She smiled, "You're most welcome, but I have to admit that I'm curious as to how I could have saved your life."

Michael left the women to check on his uncles, and Eleanor told Angela of the harrowing trip across the country from Los Angeles to Charlotte. She described the trance Max and Louis were in, the dreams, and the consistent loud voice waking her up.

Angela listened, eyes wide and mouth slightly open in shock.

Angela frowned and asked, "But why would you be targeted by evil?"

"That, Angela, is a very long story and not mine to tell unless I'm given permission." After pausing, Eleanor said, "I know what happened to you at the office. Angela, I think you have been a target of spiritual warfare just as I have, and Michael has."

"Why?" Angela asked. "Why would I be a target of spiritual warfare?"

"Because you pray," she said smiling. "You're a praying woman, and Baal doesn't like that. He hates anyone who relies on the Spirit and the power of prayer."

Eleanor squeezed Angela's hands and said, "That tantrum is over; let's finish dinner."

"Tantrum?" Angela asked, confused.

"Yes. An immature tantrum," Eleanor said smiling, "And I'm glad we could cause that much anger in the spiritual world of evil."

Angela felt confused. She understood spiritual warfare, but wondered why it was being shown so clearly in this family. There had to be more to the story. Maybe Michael could give her some more information.

Eleanor was already halfway out of the room when Angela got to her feet and followed her back to the dining room.

Eleanor smiled, "Let's finish eating. The storm has passed."

Michael watched as Max and Louis were quiet, picking at their food. He could tell they were miserable. Looking at Angela, he saw confusion, and her expression was full of questions. Eleanor, however, looked extremely pleased. Unfortunately, the happy mood of the evening had been disrupted.

After dessert, Michael said, "It's getting late. I'm going to take Angela home. I promise I will bring her back."

As they were leaving, Eleanor hugged Angela again.

"I can't tell you how delighted I am to meet you," Eleanor said, "and how glad I am that you are in Michael's life."

Angela hugged Eleanor in return. "I feel the same. I love being in Michael's life, and I'm glad I met you all."

Eleanor watched them drive away. She looked at the fallen limbs and leaves in the yard. Knowing this had been another battle, Eleanor smiled and whispered, "Prayer 5. Baal 0."

*****

On the way home, Angela looked at Michael and asked, "What happened at your family's house? I felt such a strong urge to pray when that storm started, and I was really surprised to find Eleanor in the living room praying when we walked in. After you left the room, she called the windstorm a tantrum. Why would she do that, and what did she mean by spiritual warfare at the office?"

Taking a deep breath, Michael started to explain.

"When the uncles owned the company in California, we never had a problem," he said. "It ran smoothly and made big profits. It still did when I inherited it. The problems started when I took control of the company and moved it to North Carolina. Mom is convinced the devil, Baal as she calls him, is angry that I have the company because I'm a Christian."

"So, your uncles?" she asked.

"Are not Christian," Michael answered. "Mom has been trying for years to get them to accept Christ."

"That's...." Angela trailed off.

"Scary? Unbelievable? And any other adjective you want to give it?" Michael asked.

"Yes," Angela answered.

"Your problems in the marketing department are not the only issue we've been having," Michael told her. "There have been crazy, unusual problems that we've never had before. That's why Mom thinks it's spiritual warfare, and I'm beginning to believe her."

"Do you pray at the office?" she asked.

"Yes," Michael answered. "And there have been times when I called Mom to pray for me and the company."

Angela nodded, "Well, the next time you call her to pray, let me know, too."

Michael smiled. "I'll do that."

Driving up the long driveway to the farmhouse, Michael said, "Thank you for going to dinner with me and meeting the family."

Angela smiled, "Thank you for asking."

Michael walked Angela to the front door and kissed her goodnight. Feeling the need to get closer, he kissed her again, more deeply.

"I'm falling for you so fast and so hard," he whispered. "I don't ever want to leave you."

Angela smiled and kissed him.

"I feel the same," she said softly. "I don't seem to want to do anything but spend time with you."

Hugging her tightly, Michael whispered, "I need to go. I'll see you tomorrow." He let her go and kissed her on the forehead.

Angela watched Michael walk back to his car and drive away. She turned to go into the house, her head swimming with thoughts and questions about what had happened during the visit with Michael's family.

The whole time Angela was getting ready for bed, she thought about Michael and their relationship. She was deeply in love with him. Remembering the comment he made in the restaurant about her wearing an engagement ring, Angela smiled and hoped that would happen soon.

Before climbing into bed, Angela knelt and prayed. She thanked God for his protection that evening, for Michael and for his family. Finally, she prayed that Max and Louis would accept Christ as their Savior.

CHAPTER 25

T he work week seemed to fly by for Angela. On Friday afternoon, Michael texted her.

Michael: I want to buy a boat. Want to go boat shopping tomorrow?
Angela: Uh, yes!!!!
Michael: Good. Pick you up at 9.
Angela: OK. Can't wait.

*****

Angela opened the door for Michael the next morning. He walked into the kitchen and said hello to Ray and Brenda.

"No farm work for Angela today?" he asked.

"Not today," Ray said. "Give us a few months and we'll be busy with the harvest."

Angela picked up her purse and another bag which contained a change of clothes. She said goodbye to Brenda and Ray then followed Michael out the door.

Outside, Angela stopped and stared.

"Is that your truck?" she asked. A new, black crew cab pickup was sitting in the driveway.

Michael smiled, "Yes. I needed something to pull the boat with." Michael helped Angela into the passenger's seat.

When he got behind the steering wheel, Angela said, "Leather seats, four-wheel drive, this is nice."

Michael grinned, "I'm excited about it. I understand every manly man in this state has a pickup."

Angela laughed. "We've been stereotyped! That's hilarious, but some very womanly women have them too."

Michael stopped at the end of the driveway, pulled Angela close and kissed her.

"I know a very womanly woman who drives a great big farm truck. Very sexy," he said, wiggling his eyebrows.

"Glad you think so," Angela said grinning. "Now, where are we going?"

"To buy a boat," Michael said in a serious,

matter of fact tone.

Angela laughed harder, "Alright then, on to the boat dealers."

Michael looked at boats in great detail. Angela followed him patiently, offering opinions when he asked her.

Finally, at the third dealer, Michael said, "This is it. There's a small cabin below, a canopy over the driver's seat, and comfortable seating that can even be used for fishing."

"Do you fish?" Angela asked.

"Not in a long time," Michael said. "The uncles taught me when I was a kid. They had a boat and taught me how to drive one."

Michael and Angela ate lunch at a sandwich shop while the dealer was finishing the paperwork and loading the boat onto a trailer.

"Want to take it out on the water?" he asked.

"Definitely," Angela said. "You can't buy a boat and not take it for a ride."

"I was hoping you'd say that," Michael said, smiling.

By the middle of the afternoon, Michael was lowering the boat into the water at a nearby boat ramp.

He stopped, got out and said, "When I get the boat off the trailer, will you drive the truck to my house? I'll bring the boat there."

"Oh, yeah," Angela said, "I've been wanting to drive this truck all day."

Michael laughed and shook his head. Fifteen minutes later, Angela was backing the trailer in Michael's driveway. She got out and walked down to the pier where Michael was securing the boat.

He said, "Come on up to the house for a minute. I have a map of the lake plus some drinks and snacks."

"Aye, aye, Captain," Angela said grinning.

Michael laughed, took Angela's hand and drew her to him.

He kissed her deeply and said, "I love you, Angela, and I'm changing my prediction."

"Oh?" she asked.

"This time next year you will be wearing a wedding ring," he said and kissed her.

Angela put her hand on Michael's cheek.

"I love you too, but I don't remember you asking me to marry you," she said grinning.

"Oh, I will," Michael said. "When the timing and place are right. Count on it. Will you say yes?"

"Probably," Angela said playfully and kissed him back.

The boat was fun to drive on the lake. When they got back to the pier, Michael tied the boat securely and helped Angela out. They walked hand in hand up the hill to the house.

"Dinner?" he asked.

"Yes," Angela answered. "What did you have in mind?"

"There's a great restaurant on the waterfront not far from here. Does that sound Okay?" he asked.

"Perfect. Let me get my bag from the truck. I brought a change of clothes just in case we decided to eat out." Thirty minutes later, they were dressed for dinner and driving to the restaurant.

When the hostess took them to a table near the water, Angela looked at Michael with question in her eyes.

"I made reservations," he said shrugging. Angela laughed.

Angela was wearing a sleeveless summer dress which narrowed over the shoulders. It was perfect for a summer evening.

During dinner, Michael frowned, "You got a little too much sun today."

"I'm fine," she said. "I wore sunscreen. This will be gone tomorrow."

"Good," Michael replied.

"Michael, would you like to go to church with us in the morning?" Angela asked.

"I would love to," he said smiling. "What time?"

"Be at the house by eight tomorrow morning," Angela told him. "The service starts at 8:30."

After dinner, Michael took Angela home. They ended the day sitting in the front porch swing. They talked softly, discussing their day and looking forward to the next one. Michael stood and helped Angela up, and pulled her into one last embrace.

"It's been a wonderful day, but it's getting late. I need to go," he said. "I'll see you in the morning."

Angela smiled, "OK. Drive safely." She watched him drive away and finally admitted to herself that not only was she in love with Michael Jamison, but she had been since their dinner in Durham.

CHAPTER 26

Angela was content. She was sitting in church with Michael and her parents. By the start of the last hymn, Angela felt peaceful and thankful for the way her life was unfolding. She was excited to start another work week at M & L Toys, and she felt ready to continue and strengthen her relationship with Michael.

Michael had brought a change of clothes, knowing he would be spending the day on the farm.

When they got back to the house, Angela said to Michael, "You can use the upstairs guest room to change. Would you like to take Blazer and Socks out for a ride?"

Michael smiled and said, "Yes! I was hoping we could do that."

As the two were walking toward the barn,

Michael took her hand, "I liked your church."

Angela smiled, "Good. I like it too."

He continued, "The atmosphere there is very welcoming. I never once felt like an awkward outsider. Your pastor had a great sermon, and that choir is amazing."

Angela nodded, "I agree with everything you said, and I'm particularly proud of that choir. I sang alto in it all through high school."

Michael grinned, "You sing?"

Angela rolled her eyes, "Don't get any big ideas. I said I sang alto, not soprano solos." Michael laughed.

*****

Xada had decided to check in on the Christian he was trying to get out of M & L Toys. Knowing she couldn't see him, Xada lurked behind the barn. He knew she would soon be coming to see her horses, because he had watched her often enough to know her habits.

What Xada hadn't known was that Michael was with her. When he saw them together walking to the barn, he screamed, "Nooooo!"

He was watching the auras around Michael and Angela combine when they held hands. Their relationship was getting stronger, which made him more determine to break them up.

He was angry because the closer they got to the barn, the farther away he had to retreat.

*****

Monday morning Angela walked into the marketing office. She and Michael had spent two whole days together on Saturday and Sunday, and she felt almost giddy with joy.

"Morning, Blake," she called.

Blake smiled and said, "When you get settled, come to my office."

A few minutes later, Blake and Angela sat at a small conference table fine-tuning the promotion that Angela had been working on. Blake was going to present it at a manager's meeting at ten.

"Thanks, Angela," he said. "I think this is great."

"Me, too," Angela answered. "Go wow 'em."

*****

At ten o'clock, Blake walked into the conference room. Michael was already there, seated at the head of the table. Soon everyone had arrived. Michael called the meeting to order, and each manager gave updates on his or her department.

When it was Blake's turn, he reported on the

new staff then added, "I have an idea I would like to throw out for consideration. It's a promotion for the holidays."

Blake proceeded to lay out the plan to entice customers to visit the M & L Toy stores. The promotion would start the week of Thanksgiving and run for two weeks. There would be various toys on sale, but the main feature would be the latest, newest toy in the company. The idea was that one child from each store would win one of those toys.

Blake passed out copies of the ads that he and Angela created for the promotion along with an estimated cost for the advertisements and give-aways. Everyone looked over the information then looked at Michael.

Michael looked at Blake and said, "This is good."

Looking at Sheila, he asked, "Which toy do you think we should feature?"

*****

Xada stroked Sheila's hair and whispered, "It's a terrible ad and a bad idea. They're trying to control your department."

*****

Sheila was still upset with the marketing department and didn't want anything positive coming out of there.

Feeling irritable, she said, "I don't like it. I don't think we should be giving anything away."

Michael was honestly surprised at Sheila's answer. Hiding his reaction, Michael looked at the logistics manager.

"Dan," he said, "which toy do you think we should feature?"

"The highest selling toy last year was a doll from the new line of dolls we produced," Dan said. He looked at Sheila, "It's my understanding that there are some new models coming out this holiday season along with some new accessories. I suggest we give one of those dolls and one outfit at each store for the promotion. Those dolls outsold all the trucks and cars that were bought for boys, so I don't think I'm discriminating. It's in the data. Also, the magnetic block toys sell well. I think we should feature both and let the child choose. That way we have something any child would want."

"I like this idea," Michael said. "We will do this for the brick-and-mortar stores only." He looked at Sheila, "Will you work with logistics to make sure the products are available and in every store before Thanksgiving?"

Sheila was shocked that Michael had completely disregarded her opinion. She was the one who should be deciding what toys are produced, where they should be sold, and whether or not one could be given away. Marketing and Logistics should stay out of her business. Sheila became so angry that she couldn't speak. She nodded.

Michael noticed her anger and frowned. Something was wrong. Sheila had always been a team player.

He looked at Blake and said, "I like this. Good job."

"Thank you," Blake said smiling. "I have a good team, but the idea originated from Angela. I have to give her credit."

Sheila rolled her eyes and quietly scoffed with anger.

"Sheila?" Michael asked. "Is something wrong?"

Sheila firmly said, "I don't think a nonmanagement employee should be deciding which toys to promote. Also, I don't think a nonmanagement employee has any business telling our department which toys to develop."

Michael looked at Blake who was obviously angry. The man was frowning and clenching his jaw trying to maintain calm.

Trying to control his anger, Blake said, "That's not what happened. We pitched a promotion, not the toy. Selecting which toy to promote was up to logistics and your department."

"Well, that's not what it looks like to me," Sheila said. She stood and started to leave the room.

"Sheila," Michael said.

"Yes?" she answered sullenly.

"Please have a seat. This meeting has not been adjourned," Michael said.

Sheila looked at Michael with anger and resentment but returned to her chair.

"We will move forward with this promotion," Michael said. "Logistics and Product Development will make sure the prizes are available at the stores. Marketing will do the ads and determine how the children will register for the drawing, but I want advertisement for the contest to start in early November. Let's give people something to get excited about. If no one else has anything to discuss, we will adjourn this meeting."

*****

As the managers left the conference room, Xada whispered to Sheila that she was justified in her anger and right in her opinion. That southern belle, Angela, was uppity, stepping beyond her bounds and making decisions for Sheila's department. He continued whispering more lies that Angela was arrogant and thought she was better than everyone else. Xada smiled as he realized Sheila was very receptive to his suggestions.

*****

Angela had been designing a simple registration form for children to use during the holiday contest. She rolled her shoulders and decided to go downstairs and get some coffee. Sheila was about to reenter her office when she saw Angela entering the lounge. Sheila was still stewing with anger and had reached her boiling point. She followed Angela.

Hearing the lounge door open, Angela turned around to see who had walked in.

She saw it was Sheila and said, "Hello Sheila. How are you today?"

Sheila approached Angela and shouted, "Stay out of my department!"

Angela looked surprised and confused.

"I'm sorry, but I don't know what you mean," Angela said. "I've never been in your department."

"Stop trying to decide which toys will be promoted. That is not your job," Sheila said pointing her finger angrily at Angela's face, getting too close for Angela's comfort.

Angela backed up to the cabinet and tried to stay calm.

"That's true," Angela said. "I'm not choosing any toy to promote. I help promote the toys the logistics department sends us."

"First you talk with my employees, then you pitch your very own promotion. Stay in your own lane, Missy," Sheila shouted.

"I don't understand," Angela said. "What promotion?"

"The one Blake proposed then gave you the credit for!" Sheila shouted, her voice getting louder. "That one! You may think you're all high and mighty, but you are not a manager. You're nothing, so stop trying to cross your boundaries."

Out in the lobby, Millie heard the shouting. She was so shocked she jumped out of her chair and hurried into the lounge. Opening the door, she saw Angela backed up to the cabinet, and Sheila was in her face yelling. Angela looked scared and confused while Sheila was shouting and looking like a mad bear about to attack.

"Is there a problem?" Millie asked.

Sheila swung around in anger and shouted, "This is none of your business!"

Sheila turned back to Angela and continued her rant. "How do you do it? How can you be so bad and come out looking so good?"

Angela looked at Sheila in confused shock, then she looked at Millie, pleading for her to intervene.

Millie walked over and said, "Sheila, why don't you go to your office and calm down. Then we can discuss this calmly and professionally."

"What's going on?"

Everyone turned to see Blake in the doorway. He saw Sheila's anger and her finger shaking in Angela's face. He saw Angela's wide eyed expression of confusion, and Millie was trying desperately to calm things down.

Sheila turned on Blake, shouting, "You're just as bad. You listen to her. You're all deceived by an insincere southern belle. She's impertinent and oversteps her bounds. She shouldn't be working here with her hoity toity attitude."

Sheila looked Blake in the eyes and said, "You need to get rid of her before she ruins you and your department."

Before anyone could react to the situation, Sheila stormed out of the lounge and across the hall to her office. Everyone jumped in surprise when she slammed the door.

Blake looked at Angela with concern, "Are you alright?"

Angela had moved to the table and taken a seat. Her hands were shaking.

Millie gently rubbed Angela's back and handed her a tissue.

Turning to Blake, Millie said, "I need to get back to the phones. You can handle this."

Looking at Angela, Millie said, "Angela if you need anything, just let me know. What just happened was uncalled for."

Blake quietly closed the lounge door, walked over to the table and sat across from Angela.

"Tell me what happened," he said gently.

Angela tried her best to keep from crying, but tears began to flow down her cheeks.

She took a deep breath and said, "I have no idea where her anger came from. I came in to get a cup of coffee, and she walked in right after I did. I said 'hello,' and she just laid into me out of the blue." Angela proceeded to give Blake a verbatim account of the incident.

Angela looked at Blake, "Did you give me credit for the holiday promotion during the manager's meeting?"

"I did," Blake said. "It was a team effort, but your idea."

"I think that's what she's so mad about," Angela said. "If I hadn't been involved, she may have taken it all in stride and been on board with it. I just don't understand why this has made her so angry."

Angela put her head in her hands, "I thought things like this were behind me when Evie left."

*****

Xada was perched in the darkness. He watched Blake trying to calm the upset Angela. He smiled, rubbed his hands, and patted the demon on his back. Sheila had done a good job. The praying Christian was questioning her place in the company again. Baal would be happy.

*****

"Do you want to file a complaint against Sheila?" Blake asked. "Millie and I are both witnesses."

"No," Angela answered. "I want to forget it and go back to work. I'll keep my head down and be quiet. Just don't mention my name in a staff meeting again." She stood and walked toward the door.

Blake followed Angela to the door. He was

mad, and he was frustrated. Sheila had no business attacking Angela like that, and he was almost sorry that he couldn't talk Angela into filing a complaint. He thought Sheila deserved a negative report in her employee file.

*****

Michael decided he needed a cup of coffee and walked down the stairs to the first floor. Opening the lounge door, the first thing Michael saw was Blake talking to Angela. She looked like she had been crying. It was obvious that Angela was upset, and it was all he could do to keep from taking her in his arms to comfort her.

"Is something wrong?" Michael asked.

Blake looked at Angela. He would let her answer first so he could guage how she wanted to handle things.

Angela gave Michael a weak smile.

"No. Everything is fine. I just came down for coffee," she said and held up her cup.

Angela walked past him to the elevators. Michael gave Blake a questioning look, but Blake said nothing. He shook his head, and Michael could tell he was angry. Michael watched them silently get on the elevator together.

Michael walked around to the front desk.

"Millie, do you know what happened in the lounge?" he asked. "Angela looked like she'd been crying."

"Some of it," Millie answered. "I heard shouting in the lounge and got concerned. When I opened the door, Sheila had Angela backed up against the cabinet, with her finger pointed in Angela's face and demanding Angela stay out Sheila's department. I tried to calm Sheila down, but I couldn't. When Blake walked in, Sheila started yelling at him, too. Then she stormed off to her office and slammed the door. I don't know everything that was said, but it looked to me like Sheila was out of line. The whole incident had Angela badly shaken up."

"Thank you, Millie," Michael said.

He walked into the lounge and poured himself a cup of coffee, trying to control his anger. He knew that if it had been anyone but Angela, he would have been calm and able to investigate the issue. In that moment, there was no way he could talk with Sheila or Angela without betraying emotion.

Michael knew he needed to be careful to not show favoritism, but he was finding it difficult. This was the first time he thought Angela's working at his company might be a problem.

*****

Blake followed Angela into the office. She hadn't said a word in the elevator. Angela walked to her desk and picked up the thumb drive with the latest project she had finished.

She handed it to Blake and said, "I also sent this to you in an email. I need another task. If I don't have something to do to get my mind off this, I'll be miserable."

Blake nodded. He took her to his office and gave her a list of toys going on sale before Thanksgiving.

"You can start making ads for pre-holiday sales," he said.

"Thank you," Angela said and went back to her desk.

Blake frowned with concern as he watched Angela return to her desk and start working. She hadn't deserved Sheila's anger. Part of him felt responsible because he had given Angela credit for the marketing campaign, but that was his job. He felt it was necessary to give credit where it was due. He just hoped she wouldn't come back in the morning with a resignation letter.

Chapter 27

B ack in his office, Michael began to calm down. He called Eleanor.

"Michael? What's going on?" she asked.

"I think things are getting out of control here," Michael said. "A perfectly good employee who is always a team player went ballistic on Angela. Mom, I need to investigate this, but I'm so angry that I can't. You should have seen the look on Angela's face when I walked into the lounge and her immediate boss was talking with her, trying to smooth things over."

"You're right," Eleanor said. "They're attacking Angela. My guess is that you and Angela together make a strong stand against evil. If they get her out of the company, you'll have one less person praying."

"That's what I thought, too," Michael said.

"Will you talk with Max and Louis and see if they have any insight as to what to do?" Michael paused and took a deep breath, "Mom, I think I need to explain the whole thing to Angela. She's the one being attacked, and I think she'll understand better if she knows the whole story."

"I agree," Eleanor said. "Am I right to assume that she will be part of our family in the future?"

"Yes," Michael said. "I intend to marry Angela."

"Then she needs to know," Eleanor said. "If she can put this personal attack in its proper perspective, she can deal with it and be stronger for it."

"Thanks, Mom," Michael said and ended the call.

Michael texted Angela: Are you OK?
Angela: Getting there.
Michael: Dinner at my place. I'll get takeout. Need to talk with you.
Angela: OK
Michael: Just go straight there from work. I'll leave early to get the food.
Angela: OK

Michael was relieved. At least this time she wasn't avoiding him.

*****

Max and Louis were on the patio, cleaning the fire pit. Eleanor walked over to where they were. She stood watching them.

"What's wrong, Eleanor?" Max asked.

"This is getting out of control," Eleanor said. "Angela is being attacked at the office. Ugly, vicious verbal attacks. We need to stop this."

Louis looked miserable, "I'm at a loss, Eleanor. We can't get near the company. Our being there would only strengthen Baal's minions."

Eleanor looked at her brothers with love and said, "There's a way to break free from Baal. You know it. I know you believe in God; you were Christians before you signed that contract."

Max shook his head sadly, "Signing that contract sealed our fate, Eleanor. We regret that decision every waking moment."

"Then tell God that you regret it, that you're sorry, and that you want to be in a relationship with him again. If you're sincere, there is grace and forgiveness," Eleanor said. Max looked at Eleanor, and for the first time, Eleanor saw hope in his eyes.

"You must do it soon, though," she said. "No one knows their time on earth. I wouldn't put it past Baal to take you before you have a chance to repent. No, that's not quite right. You have already repented and admitted your remorse. You just need to talk with God about it."

*****

Angela lost herself in work until she realized her coworkers were getting ready to leave. Seeing that it was five o'clock, Angela saved her progress and shut down her computer. She quietly left the building.

Michael's car was already in his driveway when Angela arrived, and she parked behind him. She sighed heavily, got out and went inside. The aroma of Chinese food met Angela when she walked into the kitchen, making her stomach growl.

"That smells wonderful," she said smiling. "I missed lunch."

Michael handed her a plate and said, "Eat."

Angela nodded and took a sample from each entrée and some rice. The two ate quietly and were comfortable with the silence. When they were finished, Angela started to put the food away and clean the kitchen.

"Leave it," Michael said. He took her hand and led her to the sofa. "I need to talk with you."

Before they sat, Michael hugged Angela, "I'm so sorry about what happened to you today. It was uncalled for." He released her and they sat down.

"I have a strange story to tell you," Michael said, "but I have permission to tell it, and I think it will put what has happened to you into perspective."

Michael proceeded to tell Angela of how Max and Louis started the company, the contract they signed, and why they retired and handed the company to Michael.

"So, first Evie and now Sheila," Michael said. "You're right; it's a personal attack, but not from them specifically. You're a strong Christian who prays, so Baal wants you out of the company. The more Christians in the company, the harder it will be for him to regain control. He has attacked you, and he attacked our profits when Evie didn't get the sales ads out in time."

Angela looked at Michael first in disbelief then in understanding.

"That makes sense now," she said. "But your uncles! They must be feeling terrible about all of this."

"They are," Michael said. "Baal never bothered the uncles until they retired. Now Baal torments them every chance he gets since he found out that I own the company. Mom has been able to protect them so far, but she is being targeted, too."

"I understand now why she said I saved her life. He's trying to kill her to weaken the protection around you, the company, and your uncles," Angela said. Her understanding turned into disgust for Baal and his tactics.

Xada watched the conversation between Michael and Angela. Angela now had the weapon of knowledge. He was angry. He was so angry that he caused the wind to start blowing, and the waves on the lake grew large, threatening to damage all the boats in the cove.

Angela looked outside, "Did you anger them by telling me? This is like the wind at your mother's house." Michael took Angela's hands and started to pray out loud.

Xada watched and screamed, "Nooooo!" The Spirit's aura around the two had strengthened as they prayed. Xada fled, and the wind and waters calmed.

Angela looked outside, "That was amazing! I wish every Christian could see just how strong the Spirit and the power of prayer are."

Michael continued to hold her hands and

looked sad.

"What's wrong?" she asked.

"I would never want to put you into a position of possible harm," he said, "but that is just what has happened."

"We can't predict the future," Angela said, "but we can reason this out. Think about it, your uncles give Baal access and the strength to fight you and try to get the company back into the hands of a non-Christian. The best solution to all of this is to convince the uncles that God's grace is for them just like the rest of us. That would be the ultimate defeat for Baal, the most humiliating loss."

Michael sat back and pulled Angela into an embrace.

He said, "Mom has been trying to get them to do that for a long time. I think they're getting closer to believing salvation is theirs. Giving the company to me is a good example of their not wanting to follow Baal anymore."

"I'm glad you told me," Angela said. "This gives me a whole different perspective as to why Evie and now Sheila were so mean. They were being used."

"Exactly," Michael said. "I wanted you to understand that it was not personal and yet it was very personal."

"I actually understood that sentence," Angela said with a mischievious grin.

Michael had his left arm around Angela and was holding her hands in his right hand. He loved her so much and was terrified of her being hurt because of the battle Baal was waging with him for control of the company. He looked outside.

"Let's go down to the dock." Michael said as he took Angela's hand and led her outside. They walked the slight slope downhill and onto the pier. At the very end was a bench, and they sat down.

The sun was setting. The western sky was a myriad of different colors ranging from pink and orange to blue and purple. A slight breeze blew, making the mid summer evening pleasant. Angela was enjoying the view, smiling in contentment.

Michael took her hand and said, "Angela, I have fallen in love with you. I don't think I could stand not having you in my life."

Angela smiled, "I love you, too, Michael, and I don't even want to think about your not being in my life."

Michael got up from the bench and knelt before Angela.

He took her hand and asked, "Angela, will you marry me?"

"Yes," Angela replied, grinning Her heart was beating fast with joy and excitement.

Michael smiled, "I had planned a much more romantic event and to present you with an engagement ring. But after what has happened, this moment felt right. What kind of engagement ring do you want?"

"Michael, this moment was perfect," Angela said. "It felt very right. I feel like our praying in the midst of evil solidified our relationship. The perfect ending to the evening was your proposal, on this pier in front of the sunset. As for a ring, I don't need one. Really, Michael, a plain gold band is all I need. Remember, I still help Dad. I would be taking an expensive ring off to work on the farm, and I would feel terrible if I lost it."

"Well, I'm still getting you a ring. You will just have to take what I choose," he said smiling.

"That will be perfect," Angela said and kissed him.

*****

Angela drove home. When she walked into the kitchen, Brenda and Ray were sitting at the table eating a piece of cake.

"How was dinner?" Brenda asked.

"Eventful," Angela said. "I need to talk with you two."

Angela sat down and told them what had happened at work and how she felt another personal attack. Then she told them the story Michael told her about his uncles, about the wind whipping the lake into white caps, about praying with Michael, and about his asking her to marry him.

Ray and Brenda were silent, taking it all in.

"Well, I guess that truly was eventful," Brenda said. "How are you feeling about all of this?"

"I'm happy about the engagement," Angela said. "The other has given me a different perspective as to why people may not like me at work. Also, I believe that the nights I woke with the need to pray was to keep Eleanor safe." Angela looked at her parents, "Honestly, I'm hoping I stay on the periphery of that problem. I don't want to go into a spiritual battle, but I think I've already been dragged into it."

Brenda took Angela's hand, "I'm pleased for you that Michael asked you to marry him. I've known for weeks that you two were in love. As for the other, let God lead you where he wants you to be, even if it is looking Baal right in the face. You're a strong prayer warrior. Baal is afraid of you. Why else would he be affecting the company, and you, that way?"

"I agree with your mother," Ray said. "I really do like Michael, and I'm glad you will be spending your life with him. If he asked you to marry him, where's an engagement ring?"

Angela laughed, "I don't think he intended to pop that question today. He was planning a nicer event for it, but things just happened. I told him I only needed a gold band, but he has insisted on a ring. So, I guess at some point I will be presented with one."

Yawning, Angela said, "I'm tired. Fighting demons and getting engaged have worn me out. Good night."

Ray and Brenda watched Angela go up the stairs.

"Well, what do you think about all that?" Brenda asked.

"I'm happy for her and Michael," Rays said. "They're a good couple, but the other? I don't know."

"I think we start praying for Angela, Michael, and his family," Brenda said. "That's the only way we can help."

CHAPTER 28

The next day, Angela smiled as she walked into the building and her office. She couldn't help but smile. Michael had asked her to marry him.

Blake looked at Angela and said, "You look happy. I was afraid you would decide enough was enough and quit."

"Nope. I'm putting yesterday in the past and moving forward. We have promo ads to get done, and I'm ready to tackle them," Angela said smiling.

Blake smiled, "Well, then, let's get to work."

*****

Baal was outside the building, "Xada, why is the Christian smiling? I thought you said you had her on the verge of quitting."

"I don't know what happened," lied Xada.

He knew exactly what had happened. He had watched her and Michael from a distance.

"Get rid of her!" Baal shouted. "I want her out of this company!"

Xada was relieved when Baal left. Now he could think.

*****

Michael sat at his desk trying his best to work. All he could think about was that Angela had agreed to marry him. He put his reports to the side and began to look at pictures of engagement rings online. His phone buzzed. There was a text from Angela.

Angela: You're invited to dinner at my house tonight. Want to go?

Michael: Of course

Angela: Good. We can go straight there from here. Told the parents about our decision. They're happy.

Michael: Good. Glad you told me that. Would hate for them to be unhappy about it.

Angela: I'm happy about it.

Michael: Me too

*****

That evening, Brenda and Ray greeted

Michael and welcomed him to the family. Michael and Angela were all smiles. Ray said grace and the four began to eat.

Ray said teasingly, "I guess we're going to have to teach Michael how to drive a tractor."

Michael smiled, "When's my first lesson? I would love to learn how to farm. "

"Really?" Ray asked.

"Really," answered Michael.

"When you have a free weekend, we'll start you out on the easy machines," Ray said.

"That's wise," Michael said grinning. "I have no idea how to do any of this." Then Michael put down his fork, looked at the others and said, "Seriously, I can't imagine a better place to live and raise children than on a farm like this."

Angela smiled, "I agree. I'm glad you think that, too."

When the meal was finished and the four were lingering over dessert, Brenda said, "Michael, I hope you don't mind, but Angela told us about the decision your uncles made and about the storm you two calmed with prayer yesterday."

Michael nodded, "That's fine. You're going to be family, too. You should know. Also, Mom and I have been begging the uncles to turn back to

God. They've been resistant, but I think they're starting to have some hope that there is a solution for their mistake."

Brenda said, "Ray and I will add you, your family, and your company to our prayers."

"Thank you," Michael replied. "I consider that a gift of love."

*****

Xada had followed Michael and Angela to the farm, but he couldn't get close enough to hear what was being said in the dining room. The aura of protection was too strong.

*****

Michael and Angela were sitting in the front porch swing and discussing their future together.

Michael asked, "Why do you never wear jewelry? I can't tell if you like gold or silver."

Angela shrugged, "I don't know. I have some necklaces I like and a bracelet or two. I do like a good watch, though. Why?"

"I'm trying to decide what type of ring you would like. The only thing I have come up with is it can't be too flashy."

Angela laughed, "That is absolutely correct. Nothing big and fancy. I told you I was perfectly happy with just a gold wedding band."

"Ah, gold, is it?" Michael asked smiling. "And unless we get married next week, you're going to wear a ring."

Angela became serious and asked, "What do I tell my coworkers if they ask? Do we keep this secret? I'm ok with that if it makes life easier at the office, but I won't keep it secret anywhere else. I'm happy and excited to be getting married to you, Michael Jamison."

"Same," Michael said and kissed her.

*****

Xada swore in frustration. He couldn't get close enough to hear their conversation.

CHAPTER 29

The next morning, the whole building was quiet. Everyone was working hard, knowing the busy holiday season would be here all too soon.

Angela felt her phone buzzing. She looked at the ID and smiled. Michael was texting.

Michael: The family wants me to bring you to their house for supper. OK?

Angela: Of course. I'll follow you from here.

Michael: Sounds good. They're happy about our decision, too.

Angela: Good. Would hate for them to not like it.

Michael: Same. Fighting the impulse to check honeymoon sights. Having trouble concentrating on work.

Angela: Be strong. You can do this. Get to work.

Laughing emoji
   Michael: OK, if I have to. See you this evening.
Heart emoji
   Angela: heart emoji

Angela smiled and returned to her computer. After another hour of work, Angela felt her stomach growl. She stood, stretched, and told Blake she was going to lunch. Taking her sandwich, fruit and canned drink to the lounge, her goal was to look at wedding gowns online while she ate.

Xada watched Angela go into the lounge. He smiled and sent a demon to convince Sheila to go across the hall again.

Sheila was irritable, almost uncomfortable in her own skin. Nothing seemed to be going smoothly, and she was still angry over the Christmas promotion to give away a toy. Maybe a cup of coffee would help.

Angela was eating when Sheila entered the lounge. She looked up, smiled and said, "Hello, Sheila. How are you today?"

"You seem content to be away from the job," Sheila said sarcastically. "Are you waiting for my staff to come back in?"

"No. I'm eating lunch. I concentrate better

when my stomach isn't growling," Angela said grinning.

Angela's smile irritated Sheila even more. Walking to the cabinet, Sheila filled a large mug with coffee. Irritation had turned to anger.

The demon had managed to get past Angela and into the lounge. He stroked Sheila's head and whispered in her ear that Angela was trying to control product development. He jabbed his fingernails into her skin, making her irritated. Sheila became angry, turned, and walked toward the table. She stumbled and spilled her hot coffee on Angela.

Angela screamed, jumped up and ran to the sink to put cold water on her burns.

Millie heard the scream and ran into the lounge. She saw Sheila looking at Angela. Coffee was all over the table and floor, and steam was rising from the pools of black liquid. Angela was crying and using the sprayer to put cold water on her burns.

Going to the sink Millie asked, "What happened? Are you alright?"

Angela was crying. "It burns, but I'll be alright."

Millie looked around. Sheila was gone.

*****

Sheila walked back into her office. Part of

her was pleased that she could put that upstart southern belle in misery, but part of her was also worried that Angela could exaggerate what happened and make it look deliberate instead of the accident that Sheila had hoped people would believe.

*****

Angela turned off the water and took the elevator to her office. She walked in and knocked on Blake's door.

Blake looked up and was immediately concerned. Angela was crying and her clothes were wet.

"What happened? Are you OK?" he asked.

"I need to go home," Angela said. "Sheila spilled hot coffee on me. I think I have some burns. At the very least I need to get dry clothes. I sprayed cold water everywhere."

Blake looked shocked, "She spilled coffee on you? Was it deliberate?"

"I don't know," Angela answered. "Right now, I don't care. I just want to get out of these clothes and put some burn cream on my arm and neck."

"Go home," Blake said. "You can work remotely this afternoon."

"Thank you," Angela said. She reached into her desk to get her purse and grimaced as the cloth of her blouse rubbed against the burns. Carrying her laptop computer, Angela left.

Blake took the stairs to the first floor and went to the lounge. He found Millie mopping the floor.

"What happened?" he asked her.

Millie replied, "I don't know. I heard Angela scream. I ran in and found her at the sink crying and spraying cold water on her arm and neck. Shelia stood at the table watching her. Sheila's coffee cup was empty, and coffee was all over the table and floor. It was hot enough that you could still see steam rising from it. I went to the sink to check on Angela, but when I turned around to talk to Sheila, she was gone."

"Thank you," Blake replied. He walked out to the elevator.

Blake walked angrily into Michael's office.

Helen looked up, frowned, and asked, "What's wrong? You look angry."

"I am. I need to see Michael," he answered.

Helen notified Michael who told her to let Blake in.

Blake walked into Michael's office. Michael saw that he was angry.

"What's happened?" he asked, pointing to a chair.

"I sent Angela home with her laptop," Blake said. "She came into my office crying, and her clothes were wet. While she was eating lunch in the lounge, Sheila came in, filled a cup with hot coffee and managed to spill it on Angela. Millie said she heard Angela scream, and when she ran into the lounge, Angela was at the sink spraying her neck and arm with cold water."

"Michael, I don't know what Evie and now Sheila have against Angela, but I'm scared this will be the last straw. I don't want to lose her, but I wouldn't blame her if she quit after this," Blake said, still angry.

Michael flushed with anger and worry. "Was it deliberate?"

"Don't know," Blake replied. "Angela said Sheila stumbled. That's all I know. Millie said when she turned to talk with Sheila, the woman was gone and had shown no sign of being concerned or sorry."

"Thank you for telling me and for caring about Angela," Michael said. "I'll deal with this, but I'm too angry at the moment. The last thing we need is one employee injuring another. Complaints are one thing, but this takes dissatisfaction to a whole different level."

Blake nodded and left the office. Michael

called Angela.

Angela was almost home when her phone rang. It was Michael. She sighed and answered.

"Hey," she said softly.

"Are you alright?" Michael asked. "Blake just told me what happened."

"I'll be fine. I need dry clothes and some burn cream, but it's not serious," Angela told him. "I will admit that it hurt pretty bad, though."

"Angela, I'm so sorry," Michael said, his voice sad and frustrated.

"It's not your fault," Angela replied. "We know who's behind this." Angela shifted uncomfortably in the driver's seat of her car.

"I'm turning into my driveway," she said. "I need to get out of these clothes and into some soft cotton. I'll call you later, but I don't think I feel like going to your family's house for supper. I'm not blaming them. I'm just pretty uncomfortable. Maybe tomorrow?"

"Don't worry. I'll take care of that. Can I come see you later?" he asked.

"Of course," Angela replied softly. "I would like that."

Michael gave a sigh of relief. "Alright. I'll see you later." Michael ended the call and immediately called Eleanor.

Eleanor answered, "Hey, Michael. What's wrong? Do you realize you never call me during the day except for a problem?"

"This is a big one," Michael said. "We won't be there for supper tonight. The woman who verbally attacked Angela just poured hot coffee on her in the lounge. Angela went home to change and get burn cream. Mom, this is a whole different level of attack. It's gone from anger and manipulation to physical injury. What do we do?"

Eleanor sighed, "I'm so sorry. Pray is all we can do, Michael. You know that."

"I know," Michael said with frustration, "but this is a new level of worry for me because I don't want employees physically hurting each other."

"No, you don't want that," Eleanor replied. "Let me tell Max and Louis. They need to know."

"Thanks, Mom," Michael said. "I need to get back to work, finish here and go see Angela."

*****

Ray and Brenda were eating lunch when Angela walked into the house. They looked up with concern.

"What happened?" Brenda asked.

"The woman who railed at me in the lounge two days ago came back to the lounge while I was eating lunch and spilled hot coffee on me," Angela said. "I need to get out of these clothes." Angela climbed the stairs to her room.

Brenda looked at Ray with concern.

She said, "This has escalated. Satan must be really angry with Angela and Michael. I'll go check on her."

When Brenda tapped on Angela's door, Angela answered, "Come in." Brenda walked in to see Angela in a pair of shorts and a tank top.

"It's not as bad as it felt," Angela told her. "Some cream with lidocaine should help."

Brenda went to the bathroom and brought some back.

"Thanks," Angela said. She took the cream and began to apply it to her neck and arms.

"Want to talk about it?" Brenda asked.

"No need," Angela replied. "We both know why it happened."

Angela looked at Brenda with tears in her eyes, "I could handle verbal attacks, but this scares me. I wasn't scared before, but I am now."

Brenda nodded, "Me, too, Angela. This scares me."

"I'm going to work here this afternoon. I think I will take snacks, lunch and water to the office and eat at my desk from now on. At least they like me in marketing," Angela said with a sad smile.

*****

Blake looked up to see Michael pushing a hand truck.

When he came out of his office, Michael saw him and said, "I have a dorm sized refrigerator/freezer, coffee maker, and coffee. Where do you want it? I don't want Angela to go back to the lounge until all this is resolved. It might be better if you don't go, either. Let your whole department use this."

Blake pointed to a corner of the room, "Put it there. There's an outlet, and it's accessible to everyone. This is a good idea, Michael. Thank you."

Michael rolled the cart to the corner.

He said, "I'm going to let you and the guys take care of this. Just put the hand trucks in Helen's office. I'll get them later."

Michael left Marketing and went down the stairs to Human Resources. George was surprised to see him, but motioned for him to come into the office. Michael closed the door and sat in the chair in front of George.

He said, "We have a big problem, George."

Michael proceeded to tell George about Sheila's verbal attack on Angela two days before and the incident in the lounge that morning. He reported that Angela had been burned and that Millie thought Sheila appeared indifferent to what happened.

Michael said, "If it had been an accident, I think Sheila would have been apologizing. She hasn't said anything to Angela. She hasn't even reported the incident. I can only assume it was deliberate. George, will you investigate the incident? Get reports from Millie, Angela, and Sheila. We can look at the story each one tells. If it's evident that Sheila did this deliberately, she will need to be terminated."

George nodded, "I agree. Yes, I'll work on this right away. The last thing we need is to set the precedence that an unhappy employee can injure another employee and get away with it."

Michael nodded and said, "I'll be out of the office. I'm going to Angela's house to see how she is and get her side of this. You can reach me on my cell phone if you need me."

Michael left the office, and George immediately opened the employee handbook and company policy to read the chapter about this type of incident. He wondered what it was about Angela Sutton that attracted the anger of her coworkers.

*****

Michael left the office and drove toward the Sutton farm. He arrived, ran up to the porch and knocked on the door.

Brenda answered, smiled, and said, "I thought you would come, but I didn't know you'd be here this soon. Angela is in the office, working. Go on in, and you're staying for supper, by the way."

Michael smiled, "Thank you."

Angela looked up when Michael walked in.

She smiled and said, "I know Blake will show this to you, but this is great. Come look."

Michael walked over, and Angela played a Christmas commercial that would start airing in early November.

"It's good," Michael said smiling.

He looked at Angela, "I'm so sorry. To know that this is escalating to physical injury scares me. Can we go outside and talk?"

"Sure," Angela said. "Let's go to the swing."

The two sat in silence for a few minutes. Angela knew Michael had something to say, so she waited patiently.

"Angela," Michael said, "I love you so much. It breaks my heart that you have been unfairly treated and now injured at my company. If you would like to work remotely for a while, I will understand."

Angela shook her head, "No. I have decided to not run away in fear. I will stand in the Word of God and tell Baal to take a hike."

Michael kissed her temple, "You're brave. Braver than I am. I wanted to lock you up and hide you from harm."

"No, not brave. Angry," Angela answered.

"Me, too." Michael looked at her arm and saw the red splotches. Some had developed small blisters. "Does it still hurt?"

"No, the cream has lidocaine. I'll be back at work tomorrow, but I may not be in very professional clothes," she said grinning.

"No worries," Michael said. "We're a toy company, remember? We don't stand on formality. I do have one thing I want to do."

"What?" she asked.

"I want you to wear an engagement ring. Let

the word go around that we're engaged. That will give you an added level of protection from the humans at least," he said.

"Are you sure?" Angela said. "I'm not afraid to keep things as they are. Announcing an engagement may bring you a whole new set of problems."

"Don't care," Michael said. "If it weren't for the uncles, I would sell everything at this point."

"Then Baal would win, and I would hate that," Angela said. "What we need is for your uncles to renew their relationship with Christ. Then they could go back to work in product development and bring the genius back to production."

"That would be the best solution," Michael said. "Mom's working on them, but the deception they believe is very strong."

"Let's change the subject," Angela said. "Let's set a date for the wedding. Honeymoon will have to wait. I have no vacation time."

"Don't care," Michael said smiling. "We're going on a honeymoon. Where do you want to go?"

Michael and Angela talked and laughed as they made plans, mostly about the honeymoon.

CHAPTER 30

A few days later, Xada was watching the office building. Baal came up behind him.

"Xada," he said, "you haven't been in to report in a while. Tell me what you have done."

Xada said, "It's hard to get close. The Christian girl has been yelled at and now burned with hot coffee. She cried then prayed," he replied disgustedly.

"But she's back," Baal observed. "Get rid of her."

*****

Max, Louis, and Eleanor had moved into their house, and most of the unpacking was done. Max and Louis were on the pier looking at the size of the boat slip. Eleanor stood watching, concerned. Her brothers had lost their joy. They seemed so sad.

Eleanor went onto the deck and sat in a chair, watching. She had a bad feeling.

Max and Louis sat on a bench at the end of the pier. The wind picked up and the water around the pier began to churn. Max and Louis looked up to see Baal. Both men were filled with a fear beyond description.

Baal was dressed in battle robes and carried a gleaming sword. He walked around the brothers, waving the sword. He got closer and closer to Max and Louis. With a twist of his wrist, his sword cut a gash in Max's arm. He turned to Louis and made a long, shallow cut on his throat below the chin. Baal backed away and watched the two men grimace in pain and grab their wounds.

"Max and Louis, you left California," he said arrogantly, still waving the sword. "You left the place where I wanted you to be and came to this infernal Bible belt. Well, you can redeem yourselves. I want you to get rid of that praying girl that is so close to Michael. I don't care how, but you get her out of the company. You can kill her for all I care. I want her gone!"

Eleanor noticed the change in wind and felt

the drop in temperature. Max and Louis were sitting still, staring into space. Eleanor began to pray out loud.

Baal looked up at the house and yelled, "Get rid of that praying woman, too!" Then he disappeared.

Eleanor ran to the pier. Max and Louis looked at her.

"What happened?" she asked. Looking at her brothers she exclaimed, "You're bleeding! Did Baal do that?"

Max nodded and said, "He was here."

"What did he want? And how did he make you bleed?" she asked incredulously.

"He's angry that the company was moved from California, and he wants us to get rid of Angela," Louis said.

"What did he mean by that?" asked Eleanor, concerned.

Max replied, "He said out of the company." Max hesitated then said, "He said we could kill her if we wanted to. He wants us to get rid of you, too."

Eleanor looked horrified. "Kill her? He wants you to kill her? You can't do that! As for me, there's no surprise there, we've been down that road. Angela went back to work today. That's why he's mad, but you can't kill her!"

Max and Louis held up their hands and shook their heads vigorously.

"We would never harm Angela," Louis said. "We will take our reckoning before we harm you, Angela or Michael."

The three were quiet. Max looked at Eleanor. His expression was so sad it broke Eleanor's heart.

Max said, "I'm so sorry we have brought fear and danger to the people we love. We never wanted that."

Eleanor smiled sadly, "I know. Baal is finally showing you his true colors. He's selfish, arrogant, and evil. You can get out of this. I think that's why he's so mad. I think he's afraid you're going to do the one thing that will make him lose you. He's afraid you will renew your relationship with Christ. You had one once. Jesus is just waiting for you to admit your mistake and your remorse for it and ask to be in his presence again."

"Do you think so?" Louis asked.

"I know so," Eleanor said smiling. "Let's go clean those cuts."

Walking back to the house, Eleanor smiled and whispered, "Prayer 6, Baal 0."

*****

Angela went back to work the next day. She got her lunch from the refrigerator and ate at her desk.

Blake walked over, "If you're going to work through lunch, feel free to leave a little early."

Angela smiled, "Thanks. I might do that on occasion. Remember, we're still working short staffed. Any prospects?"

"One," Blake replied. "He has experience with video and editing. He's interviewing early next week."

"That sounds good," Angela replied. She watched Blake walk back to his office then felt her phone buzz with a text.

Michael: I have reservations for dinner.
Angela: Yay. I'm all for dinner.
Michael: Good. I'll pick you up at your house at six. Reservations at seven.
Angela. Nice or casual?
Michael: Nice
Angela: OK. I'll be ready.

Angela smiled. She thought that maybe

tonight the ring would appear.

*****

That evening, Michael parked at a waterfront restaurant at the lake.

Angela smiled, "I've heard this is a great restaurant. Have you eaten here?"

"No," he answered. "Have you?"

"Not yet," she said smiling. "I can't wait to try it."

The atmosphere was quiet and romantic. They had a table at a window with a view of the lake.

Angela said, "This is lovely. Good choice."

When they had finished their entrees, Michael ordered one dessert with two spoons. When they finished eating, Michael pushed the bowl to the edge of the table.

He took Angela's hand and asked, "With all that's happened, you haven't changed your mind about marrying me, have you?"

"No. You asked, I said yes, and I'm holding you to it," Angela answered smiling.

Michael grinned, took the ring from his pocket and slipped it on Angela's left ring finger.

"It's official," he said. "You're engaged to me."

Angela looked at the ring. A row of small diamonds sat low on a narrow band of gold.

"This is beautiful. I love it." She looked at Michael, "I love you."

"I love you, too," Michael answered. He stood, "Come on. Let's go. If I don't get you somewhere that I can kiss you, I think I will howl."

Angela laughed. As soon as they were in Michael's car, he leaned over and gently kissed her.

"How soon can we get married?" he asked.

"How about January?" she asked. "That gives us time to plan and also to help Dad with the harvest which is coming up soon."

Michael smiled, "I'm going to be planning my life around planting and harvesting, aren't I."

"I'm afraid so," Angela replied, grinning. "Do you mind?"

"Not a bit," Michael said and kissed her. "There are great vacation destinations in the winter."

"Let's go home," Angela said. "I want to show off my ring!"

*****

The next morning, Angela sat at her desk, looking at her ring and smiling.

"What has you so happy?" Blake asked.

Angela said, "Let's go to your office. I have news."

Blake looked puzzled but said, "Alright."

When they were seated, Angela showed him her ring. "I'm engaged to be married."

Blake smiled.

"To Michael Jamison," she said with a sheepish look.

Blake laughed. "I wondered. I told you; I don't care if you marry him, you can't leave this department."

Angela smiled, "I don't want to. We aren't making any big announcement, but I thought you should know. Remember, we knew each other before I started working here."

"How did you meet, if you don't mind my asking?" Blake said.

Angela gave him a sheepish grin. "I went to Long Beach to interview because I had a long weekend and wouldn't have to miss work. We had seats together on the long flight back to Charlotte. We clicked. He didn't tell me until two days later who he really was."

Angela looked at Blake, "Let me know if this is going to be a problem. I will quit before I give up Michael. That's how much I love him."

"No worries, Angela. I think we get along well enough that your relationship with my boss shouldn't be too much of a problem," he said grinning.

"Oh, you. Stop joking. It'll be fine," Angela said.

"Yes, it will," Blake said. "No worries and congratulations."

Angela went back to her desk and texted Michael.

Angela: Hey, I told Blake and showed him the ring.

Michael: And?

Angela: He's good with it. Said congratulations and that I couldn't leave the department. Blushing smile emoji

Michael: Good. Mom called. Dinner there OK?

Angela: Yes. I will try to keep my clothes dry this time. Laughing emoji

Michael: Not funny Didn't like you hurt.

Angela: No worries. I'll follow you to their house. Got to get back to work. The owner of this company is demanding.

Michael: Yes, demanding kisses from you.

Angela: Good. Likewise. Gotta go.

CHAPTER 31

Angela followed Michael to his family's new home and parked behind behind him in the driveway.

When she got out of the car, she said, "This place is huge! Your house would fit in here twice."

Michael said, "The uncles and mom all want their own suites with bedroom, bath, and sitting area. Takes a big house to accommodate that. I haven't been here yet. I guess we get to see it together."

Angela looked at Michael and grinned, "Plenty of room for the children to run around when we need them to babysit."

Michael grinned, took her hand, and rang the doorbell. He opened the door and called, "Mom!"

"In the kitchen," Eleanor called. "Just come down the hall."

Michael and Angela walked into a large living area that had the kitchen, dining area, and great room.

"This is beautiful!" Angela exclaimed.

"We like it," Eleanor said. "I have a suite on this floor. Max and Louis have rooms on the second. There is a living area, bedroom and bath on the basement level."

Eleanor looked at Angela, "How are you feeling? I'm so sorry you were injured at work."

Angela smiled, "I'm fine."

Max and Louis entered from the deck.

Max called, "Steaks are ready!"

"Everything else is on the table," Eleanor said. "Let's eat."

When everyone was seated, Eleanor said, "Let's join hands." Max and Louis looked uncertain.

"You, too," Eleanor said.

Eleanor said a blessing and added a special prayer for protection during the meal with the request that Max and Louis see the light and renew their relationship with God.

When she had finished praying, Eleanor looked at her brothers and asked, "What happened during the prayer?"

"I felt a strange, heavy sensation in my chest," Louis said. "I've never felt that before." Max nodded in agreement.

Eleanor smiled, "That's God knocking at your heart. Let's eat."

During the meal, everyone talked, laughed, joked and told stories about Michael when he was growing up. Angela loved hearing everything they said.

*****

Xada watched the group around the table. He was suddenly afraid. He couldn't get close enough to hear what was happening, but when Max and Louis joined hands with the others, he saw a spark of aura around them during the woman's prayer. Thank goodness it died.

As the meal progressed, Xada watched joy fill Max and Louis. This was not good. He sent a demon for Baal. The two men were getting too close to making a decision to return to God. Baal needed to take them tonight. Soon hundreds of demons were coming to the house and landing in the trees. They would be there to rejoice when Baal took the two souls.

*****

Brenda and Ray Sutton were eating dinner. Both were suddenly struck with the need to pray.

Brenda looked at Ray, "Angela's in danger. She's at their house."

Ray nodded. The two joined hands and began to pray for their daughter and the family of her fiancé. They earnestly prayed that Max and Louis would return to Christ.

*****

Eleanor went into the kitchen to get dessert. A movement outside the window caught her attention. When she looked out, she could see nothing out of the ordinary, but a dark cloud was forming in the north. The trees started shaking and loosing leaves like they were filled with birds, but they weren't, and the wind was not blowing. A cold feeling of dread and understanding filled Eleanor's chest.

Running back into the dining room, Eleanor shouted, "Everyone get up. Go into the den."

She put Max and Louis in the center while she, Michael, and Angela held hands and formed a circle around them.

Eleanor said, "Max, Louis, you have repented. You need to tell God and request to be accepted into his presence."

She looked outside, and said loudly and urgently, "Now! I'm sure Baal is coming, and I'm confident he has a legion of demons with him." Eleanor began to pray out loud for protection from Baal. Michael joined her.

The wind started to blow and get steadily stronger. Dark clouds formed and began to descend to the ground, causing a strange fog. Outside, the demons were celebrating loudly making a shrieking sound in wind. Eleanor heard the eerie sound and continued to pray.

Outside the house was chaotic and frightening. Inside the house, Eleanor and Michael's prayers fell into the background. Angela felt like time was standing still. She could hear Eleanor and Michael praying, but she was focused intently on Max and Louis.

She smiled and said quietly, "Now is your time. Max and Louis, do you believe in God and his son, Jesus, and that Jesus died for your sins?"

"Yes," they both answered.

"Would you like to return to a relationship with Christ?" she asked.

Max and Louis looked at each other.

With tears streaming down their faces, they looked at Angela and answered, "Yes."

"Tell him," Angela said gently.

Max and Louis dropped to their knees. They prayed in anguish at their remorse for believing Baal and signing the contract. They prayed their desire for forgiveness and acceptance back into God's grace and his presence. They prayed their desire for a renewed relationship with him.

"Nooooo!" screamed Baal.

His army of demons were surrounding the house, getting ready to enter and take the souls of Max and Louis. Suddenly, Baal watched an army of heavenly warriors with flaming swords begin fighting their way to the house. The battle was fierce, but Baal saw that his army was no match for the heavenly angels.

The wind was blowing, and rain was falling sideways. Large waves formed white caps on the lake. Baal was angry. He picked up a tree and threw it into the house, hoping to hit the people inside. He wanted Max and Louis before they had a chance to renew a relationship with God.

Michael saw the large tree starting to fall on the house.

"Run to the back!" he yelled.

The group reached the back door just as the tree crashed into the front of the house. Suddenly everything was still and quiet. Neighbors rushed over to see if Eleanor, Max, and Louis were alright. Everyone in the neighborhood went outside to check their homes and piers for damages after the strange sudden microburst of wind and rain.

Max and Louis went to the living room to assess the damage. Eleanor came up to them.

"How are you?" she asked.

They turned to her and smiled.

"Amazing. Peaceful," Max said.

"Joyful. I feel lighter than I have in decades," Louis said.

Eleanor smiled, "I'm so glad and relieved. Now I can spend eternity with you."

Both men turned to Angela, hugged her and thanked her for her gentle prodding and leading them back to Christ.

She smiled and hugged each one.

"I'm so glad," she said. "Now I get the chance to know you, and you will get the chance to know our children when they come."

The five stood in the middle of the debris and held hands. Michael, Angela and Eleanor listened as Max and Louis prayed prayers of thanksgiving, praise and gratitude.

*****

Baal hovered at a distance. He had lost his recruits. They both had the aura of Christians. The strength of the spirit and the presence of heavenly angels were so strong over the house that he had to retreat another mile away.

Angry, Baal howled his way back to Washington, causing weather disturbances as he went. Xada and the demons quietly followed, not wanting to get his attention.

*****

Later, Angela and Michael sat at the Sutton's kitchen table telling Brenda and Ray everything that happened.

"Ray and I felt the need to pray," Brenda said looking at Michael. "It was so urgent that we were afraid for you, Angela, and your family."

"Thank you," Michael said. "I know your prayers helped protect us, but I think they led Angela to say the right thing at the right time to encourage Max and Louis."

The four sat around the kitchen table and held hands while Ray thanked God for his blessings and protection.

*****

Everything was quiet. Max and Louis had taken pictures of the damage to the living room, deck, and yard. Neighbors with chain saws had removed the tree from the house and helped them place plastic tarps across the damaged roof and windows.

Eleanor relived the events of the night and smiled. She didn't care about the damage. What mattered was that Max and Louis had renewed their relationship with Christ and were Christians again.

She whispered aloud, "Prayer 7. Baal 0."

Eleanor smiled. Seven, God's perfect number, and salvation was God's perfect plan.

CHAPTER 32

The next morning, Angela walked into the M & L Toy Company headquarters. Something was different. The atmosphere was different, lighter. She took the elevator to the third floor, but instead of going to marketing, she turned and walked to Michael's office. Helen was already at her desk.

"Can I help you?" Helen asked.

"Is Michael in?" Angela asked.

Michael heard Angela outside at Helen's desk. He got up and opened his door.

"Angela? Is everything alright?" he asked. "Come into the office."

Angela walked into the office. Michael closed the door and hugged Angela.

"What's wrong?" he asked.

"Nothing," Angela replied. "Do you feel a difference in the atmosphere?"

Michael smiled, "I do. This company no longer belongs to Baal."

"He lost!" Angela said smiling. She frowned, "but do you think he will try to retaliate?"

Michael shrugged, "It won't work. He lost. The uncles and the company are under God's influence. Baal may as well move on." Michael opened the door. "I'll walk you to your office."

As they walked by Helen's desk, Michael said, "Helen, this is Angela Sutton, a very creative marketing employee and my fiancé."

"It's nice to meet you, Helen," Angela said with a smile.

Helen looked surprised then smiled.

"It's nice to meet you too, Angela," she said. "This is marvelous! A wedding is coming."

She looked at Michael, "I hope we're all invited."

Angela laughed, "You will be, I promise."

Michael's cell phone buzzed. He looked at the text and smiled.

"Let's go downstairs," he said to Angela. "Max and Louis are here. They want to go to work."

EPILOGUE

Michael and Angela were married in January. Both Max and Louis stood with Michael as well as Peter, his friend from college and company colleague. Angela's two cousins and one friend stood with her. Most of the employees at the office were in attendance.

*****

Baal watched angrily from a distance. Those people and this community were too strong in the Spirit. Unfortunately, there were hundreds of communities like this across the country. He needed to change his tactics if he was going to win this country for himself. He went back to Washington, summoned his leadership team and began to plan. It was time to neutralize the praying people.

ALSO BY A. K. GENTRY

An Awkward Inheritance, Whitlow Series

An Unlike Partnership, Whitlow Series

Coming Soon

An Unforeseen Danger, Whitlow Series

Unprepared, Forewarned Series